COUNTDOWN TO
DANGER
CHOOSE YOUR OWN ENDING!

Ten years ago some amazing wordsmiths very patiently taught me almost everything I know about being a writer.
Thanks to Kate Forsyth, Justine Larbalestier, David Levithan, Tara Moss, Matthew Reilly, Scott Westerfeld and most of all, Claire Craig.

Scholastic Canada Ltd.
604 King Street West, Toronto, Ontario M5V 1E1, Canada

Scholastic Inc.
557 Broadway, New York, NY 10012, USA

Scholastic Australia Pty Limited
PO Box 579, Gosford, NSW 2250, Australia

Scholastic New Zealand Limited
Private Bag 94407, Botany, Manukau 2163, New Zealand

Scholastic Children's Books
Euston House, 24 Eversholt Street, London NW1 1DB, UK

www.scholastic.ca

Library and Archives Canada Cataloguing in Publication

Heath, Jack, 1986–, author
Deadly heist / Jack Heath.
(Countdown to danger)
Previously published: Scholastic Australia, 2017.
Issued in print and electronic formats.
ISBN 978-1-4431-6307-1 (softcover).--ISBN 978-1-4431-6308-8 (HTML)
1. Plot-your-own stories. 2. Choose-your-own stories.
I. Title.
PZ7.H35Dea 2017   j813'.6   C2016-907983-X
C2016-907984-8

First published by Scholastic Australia Pty Limited, 2017.
This edition published by Scholastic Canada Ltd., 2017.
Text copyright © 2016 by Jack Heath.
Illustration and design copyright © 2016 by Scholastic Australia.
Cover by Steve Wells Designs.
Additional illustrations: Police car with lights © u3d | Shutterstock.com; Image of dollar rain © Revenant | Shutterstock.com; Light trails on modern building backgrounds: 86409772; 161893115; 85757920 © zhangyang13576997233 | Shutterstock.com; Office vector house illustration © petovarga | Shutterstock.com; Red real laser beam on black background © Michal Vitek | Shutterstock.com; Metallic security shield © Tribalium | Shutterstock.com; Helicopter in flight © Baldas1950 | Shutterstock.com; Asphalt road and modern city © gui jun peng | Shutterstock.com; House building and city construction © Scanrail1 | Shutterstock.com; Soldier silhouettes and arms © lapi | Shutterstock.com; Dark storm clouds © Dudarev Mikhail | Shutterstock.com; Stage spotlight with laser rays © snvv | Shutterstock.com; Panoramic skyline and buildings with empty road © zhu difeng | Shutterstock.com; Black Van © Trimitrius | Shutterstock.com; Concert lighting against a dark background © Skylines | Shutterstock.com; Traffic in Hong Kong at night © ESB Professional | Shutterstock.com; Grunge border © Rochakred | Dreamstime.com; Digital timer © milmirko | iStockphoto.com; Digital clock © Samarskaya | iStockphoto.com; Urban Skyline © Bakal | iStockphoto.com.
5 4 3 2 1   Printed in Canada 139   17 18 19 20 21

JACK HEATH

COUNTDOWN TO DANGER

CHOOSE YOUR OWN ENDING!

DEADLY HEIST

Scholastic Canada Ltd.
Toronto New York London Auckland Sydney
Mexico City New Delhi Hong Kong Buenos Aires

30:00

The black van screeches to a stop right in front of you. The side door rolls open. Three men and one woman leap out. All of them have black boots, mirrored sunglasses and knit hats. One of the men wears grey overalls with *SPENCER'S AIR CONDITIONING REPAIR* written on the back. The other three are dressed in black.

There's something frightening about them. You take a step backwards. They move like soldiers and they're bigger than you. The woman has a scar, which runs from her eyebrow down to the corner of her mouth. One of the men has a picture of a knife tattooed on his muscular arm. Another has a large signet ring on one of his fingers. The guy in the overalls has a silver tooth.

They run straight past you and disappear into the HBS bank. The van zooms away, leaving a haze of exhaust in the cold morning air. The echoes of the engine die away.

You look around. Cars cruise along the street. Trucks roll in and out of the warehouse across the road. It's barely light — at this time of year the sun doesn't rise until almost eight — but surely someone else must have seen the black van and its sinister passengers.

If anyone did, they don't seem to care.

Pedestrians wander past you, heads down. No one has reacted.

The bank doesn't look like a bank. If not for the ATM-finder app on Kye's phone, you would have walked right past it. There are no signs on the concrete walls. Shutters cover the few windows. But it's open, which most banks aren't when it's this early.

Kye entered a minute ago to deposit some cash. He said he'd be right back. What if he meets the four strangers from the van? What if they are dangerous?

You whip out your phone and call Kye. But the call doesn't connect, not even to his voicemail. Weird.

You could phone the police. But what would you say? It's not a crime to wear black, or to have a scar, or to run into a bank. The van might have been speeding, but that's it. The cops will think it's nothing. It probably is nothing.

Maybe you should quickly go into the bank, grab Kye and get out. Then you can both decide what to do. You might even get a better look at the four strangers. You could see something that proves they're innocent . . . or they're not.

If you go into the bank, go to page 5.
If you call the cops, go to page 10.

20:59

"Jacob," you say.

"Full name," Miss Scarlet says.

"Jacob Catton," you stammer.

She holds out her hand. "Let's see your ID, 'Jacob Catton.'"

All you have is a student card. You hand it over with a trembling hand.

She looks at it, thinking, and then pockets it. "OK," she says. "The bankers should be calling the police right now. When the cops arrive, they'll call the phone in the staff room. When it rings, you're going to pick it up and say exactly what I tell you to. One word wrong and your little friend here gets it."

She points the laser at Kye. The colour drains from his face.

"You don't have to threaten him," you say quickly. "I'll do whatever you want."

"Yes," she says. "You will. Now—"

A shrill whistle cuts through the air. Miss Scarlet turns to look at the melted hole in the glass at the counter.

"Something's wrong," Mr. Sharp says.

Miss Scarlet shushes him. They both move away towards the counter, out of your sight.

While they're distracted, you scan your surroundings, looking for a way out. The air conditioner catches your eye. It's not properly attached to the wall — and you can see a vent behind it. The vent looks just big enough to crawl through. That must be why Miss Scarlet didn't want you near it.

Can you and the other hostages get out of sight before the bad guys turn around?

If you lead the other hostages into the vent, go to page 12.

If you don't risk it, go to page 16.

26:32

You look both ways and then run into the HBS bank. A sliding door lets you into a small foyer, with a security camera and a pair of ATMs. No people. This room is just an airlock, keeping the winter out.

A second door opens and you slip through into a larger room. Dotted lines on the soft grey carpet show customers where to go. One woman is selecting options on a touchscreen. A printer below it spits out a numbered ticket. The woman takes it and sits down on an orange bench next to two other people, both with tickets in their hands.

Kye — a gangly boy with curly blond hair and glasses — is at one of the counters, chatting with a bank teller. He always talks too much, especially to people who are just trying to do their jobs in peace.

You wonder if the teller can even hear him. There's a thick window between him and her. A sign says, *WARNING! SECURITY SHUTTER RISES QUICKLY.*

The big guy with the knife tattoo — in your head you call him Mr. Sharp — is standing near the door. Not blocking it, exactly. Like everyone else in here, he looks like he's waiting for something. Nervously, you walk past him towards Kye.

One of the other men — the man with the signet ring — looms next to the orange bench, a grim smile on his face. He doesn't appear to have a ticket.

The woman with the scar stands in a corner, the hood of her jacket pulled over her head. She's directly under a security camera — in its blind spot.

You can't see the man with the silver tooth and the overalls anywhere.

Kye finishes talking to the teller, takes his receipt through the gap under the glass and starts walking to the exit. He slows down when he sees you.

"Hey," he says. "You get lonely out there?"

"Hurry up," you say.

A bell rings and a message flashes up on a screen: *NOW SERVING 81 AT COUNTER 2.*

One of the people on the bench — a middle-aged woman wearing a fluffy scarf — stands up. The guy with the signet ring peels himself off the wall and approaches the second counter, where Kye just was.

The woman with the scarf looks down at her ticket, confused.

You and Kye walk towards the exit.

"Get ready to run," you whisper. "I think those guys are robbers."

"They're *what?*" Kye asks, too loudly.

Mr. Sharp's eyes narrow.

Someone screams. You turn in time to see the guy with

the signet ring throw a grenade towards the bank teller.

She reacts immediately, kicking something under the counter. A steel shutter shoots upwards, covering the glass. A deafening alarm shrieks.

With a loud clank, Mr. Signet's grenade expands into a giant ball of crooked spikes. The spikes get jammed between the shutter and the ceiling, stopping it from rising all the way. About half a metre of glass is exposed.

Before you can run, another shutter crashes down over the exit. You and Kye are trapped!

The woman with the scar pulls out a futuristic-looking weapon. She points it at the security camera above her head and pulls the trigger. A purple laser shoots out of the muzzle and bores a hole right through the camera. She steps out of the way in time to avoid the falling chunks of blackened metal and plastic.

Then she takes off her hood and her hat, revealing a mane of blood-red hair.

"You've all seen movies," she says. "You know what a bank robbery looks like."

She tosses the laser to Mr. Signet. He climbs up onto the counter and starts melting the exposed glass.

"In twenty-five minutes you all get to walk out of here," says Miss Scarlet — the redhead with the scar. "No one is going to get hurt, because no one is going to do anything foolish. Right?"

Everyone stares at her in terrified silence.

"Right?" she says again.

You nod hurriedly. Kye and the other customers do the same. But you wonder if she's telling the truth. She melted the camera so it wouldn't see her face. You and all the other customers have seen it. Will she really let you go?

"You're all going to sit over there." She points to the corner. "Backs against the wall, hands where I can see them."

Mr. Signet has finished cutting through the glass with the laser. The edges of the hole glow like hot coals. He throws the weapon back to Miss Scarlet. Then he pulls some gloves on, clambers through the gap and disappears.

You and the rest of the hostages shuffle over towards the wall. Miss Scarlet watches you closely.

She holds up a device that looks like a cross between a Wi-Fi router and a walkie-talkie. Antennas bristle from the top and red lights blink along one side. "This is a multi-band frequency jammer," she continues, "with a range of sixty metres. Your cellphones won't work in here, so don't try."

That explains why you couldn't call Kye from outside. You look at him. His eyes are wide.

The alarm suddenly stops. Mr. Signet must have found a way to switch it off.

Miss Scarlet holds up the laser. "You've just seen

what this does to three inches of bulletproof glass," she says. "Do you know what else it can do?"

No one says anything.

"Behave yourselves," Miss Scarlet says, "and you won't find out. You!"

She points at you. Your heart leaps into your mouth.

"Move away from the AC," she says.

You're sitting right next to the air conditioning unit. It isn't switched on. It doesn't even look like it's attached to the wall properly — the underside rests on the floor. You scoot away from it. Miss Scarlet must not want you near it because then you wouldn't be visible from the counter.

"What's your name, kid?" she asks.

If you say "Jacob," go to page 3.
If you say "Brianna," go to page 121.

26:32

You dig out your phone and dial emergency services. Once again, the call doesn't connect. You check the screen. The signal strength is good. There must be something wrong with your phone.

You look around. Maybe a pedestrian will let you borrow their phone.

And then you see a police officer, standing on the street corner near a patrol car.

Unable to believe your luck, you run over to him. He's observing the street very carefully, perhaps looking for someone in particular. He's clean shaven, with hazel eyes and dirty blond hair peeking out from under his police hat.

"Excuse me."

He looks at you, but doesn't say anything.

"I think that bank is getting robbed," you say.

His eyes widen. He looks at the bank, then at you. He scans the street again.

"Four suspicious looking people just went in," you continue. "And then their van sped off."

"I see," he says. "Suspicious looking? In what way?"

Feeling silly, you say, "They were wearing black and they were running."

The officer smiles slightly. "That doesn't sound like anything to worry about."

"Come with me," you say. "I'll show you."

"No, you go home," he says. "I'll keep an eye on things here."

Kye could be in danger, but this police officer isn't taking you seriously. Maybe he would listen if you exaggerated a little bit.

If you tell him the robbers had weapons and ski masks, go to page 107.
If you go back to the bank and try to sneak in, go to page 111.

18:37

As quietly as you can, you lift the air conditioning unit away from the wall. It makes a faint scraping sound, but Miss Scarlet and Mr. Sharp don't seem to notice. You can hear them hissing instructions through the hole in the glass.

The other hostages stare at you in silent horror. They think you're going to get them into trouble. Ignoring them, you shift the air conditioning unit out of your way, exposing the air vent.

It's narrower than it looked at first. But it's too late for second thoughts. You beckon to the others and wiggle into the darkness.

The aluminum walls are tight around your shoulders. It's hard to crawl quickly or quietly. Your knees keep getting jammed up. But soon you're in far enough that there's room for Kye to crawl in behind you.

"You're crazy," he whispers.

Ignoring him, you keep pulling yourself into the gloom. You start to feel claustrophobic. There's barely enough room to lift your head, let alone turn around. For an air vent, there doesn't seem to be much air.

Hands and shoes shuffle and thump behind you. It sounds like some other hostages — two women and a man — have decided to follow you and Kye into the tunnel.

There's a sharp corner up ahead. If you can get around it, the woman with the laser won't be able to target you from the entrance. But it's going to be a tight squeeze.

You roll onto your back and brace your arms against the ceiling so you can squirm around the corner. The sharp edge scrapes your hip and stomach, but you make it. There's a grill in the floor, leading to what looks like a room below.

But in the shadows on the other side of the grill, you can see the fourth robber. The man with the silver tooth. That must be why he was wearing the air conditioner repair overalls — so he could take the unit off the wall and crawl into the vent without anyone stopping him.

He hasn't seen you yet. He's fiddling with a phone. Perhaps you can push through the grill and get into the room below before he spots you. Or maybe you should sneak up on him and try to snatch the phone out of his hands, so he can't warn the other robbers.

If you push through the grill to escape into the room below, turn to page 19.

If you charge at the man with the silver tooth, turn to page 24.

12:09

"**H**elp everyone else get down from the vent," you tell Kye. You run over to the wall and wrench the fire axe off the cradle.

An alarm shrieks. It's a harsh beeping sound — different from the shrill jingle of the robbery alarm. You ignore it and run up the first flight of stairs towards the door with the security shutter.

"Quick!" Kye yells to the others. "Jump!"

You hope he can get everyone into the stairwell before Mr. Silver wakes up, or one of the other robbers finds you all.

The axe is much heavier than they look on TV — actors must use plastic axes. You swing it with all your might.

The blade slams into the shutter. It doesn't break through the steel, but leaves a shallow dent. You raise it and swing again.

Crash! The shutter still holds.

"Watch out!" Kye cries.

You whirl around. The other three hostages are cowering in the corners of the stairwell. Miss Scarlet is hanging upside down out of the vent, holding her laser. She takes aim at you.

You turn to run farther up the stairs—

And you crash into Mr. Sharp. He's come down from the floor above. He looks furious.

He wrenches the axe out of your grip.

You raise your hands. "No, no!"

He swings the axe towards you but you dive backwards before he can strike—

And your feet come down on a step that isn't there.

You jumped too far. You're falling. Your arms pinwheel as you tumble backwards towards the concrete floor ...

SMACK!

THE END.

To try again, go back to page 12.

18:37

You scoot away from the air conditioning vent, so the robbers don't notice that it's open. You might need to use it later.

"What do we do?" Kye whispers.

"They won't hurt us," you say. "Why would they? They'd get more jail time if they did, right?"

"So . . . what do we do?" Kye says again.

"Nothing. We sit tight. The police will catch the robbers, or they'll get away — either way, we're fine. As long as we don't make them mad."

You sound more confident than you feel. But Kye isn't fooled. He's known you for a long time.

Miss Scarlet returns. "Come with me," she says.

Everyone starts to get up.

"No," she says, and points a finger at you. "Just you."

So much for sitting tight. With one last frightened glance at Kye, you stand up and follow Miss Scarlet.

A hidden door is built into the wall next to the counter. The guy with the ring, Mr. Signet, has opened it from the other side. Miss Scarlet pushes you through the doorway into the room beyond.

This is the part that customers aren't supposed to see. A table is littered with receipts, business cards and empty coffee mugs. Someone has scribbled a message on a sticky note: *New code is 137. Don't forget!*

No sign of the staff.

A cart is parked crookedly in the corner, overflowing with bundles of cash wrapped in rubber bands.

The robbers ignore the cash completely. They also ignore the door marked *PANIC ROOM.* That must be where the staff escaped to.

Miss Scarlet leads you over to the telephone — an old-fashioned plastic landline with a cord. "When the police call," she says, "tell them no one has been harmed, and no one *will* be harmed, so long as the police stay away. We will be out of here in ten minutes. We'll take one hostage with us. The hostage will be released once we've reached a safe location."

This is a lot to take in. "Why don't you talk to them?" you ask.

"Don't ask questions," Miss Scarlet says. Perhaps she thinks they'll recognize her voice.

Mr. Signet leans over to her. "I can't get the vault open," he says.

"There's a key in the manager's desk."

"I got it already." Mr. Signet holds up a long key. "But there's a keypad as well and the combination you gave me didn't work."

"Try it again," Miss Scarlet says.

Mr. Signet walks over to a massive steel door set in a

concrete wall and locked with dozens of electronic bolts. He inserts the key into an invisible hole and punches numbers into a keypad below. The keypad beeps angrily.

"They must have changed the combination," he said. "If I get it wrong once more, it will lock us out for twelve hours."

Miss Scarlet thinks for a moment and then turns back to you.

"New plan," she says. "When the police call, order them to get the vault combination from the security company. Tell them we have five hostages."

If you know the code for the vault, turn to that page.
If you don't, go to page 59.

13:51

You push down on the grill. It doesn't pop out of the frame.

You push harder. The grill still doesn't come out, but this time it groans loudly. Mr. Silver — the man with the silver tooth — looks up.

You stare at one another, frozen in mutual horror for a second. Then you start to scramble backwards around the corner. Mr. Silver drops his phone and lunges forward to grab you—

Then the grill collapses under his weight. He screams as he falls out of the vent and disappears into the darkness below. An ugly thud echoes through the chamber.

Motion-activated lights flicker on. Mr. Silver hasn't fallen very far. He's landed on a concrete floor next to a set of stairs, going up. His eyelids are flickering. He's stunned, or concussed.

The other robbers probably heard the scream. It won't take them long to work out where it came from.

"Hurry!" you hiss. You drop down onto the floor next to Mr. Silver and drag him out of the way so the others can climb down.

You find yourself on the bottom floor of a stairwell. Old wooden pallets are stacked in the corner. A fire axe is mounted on the wall. You're below ground level, so the only way out is up the stairs.

There's a door on the first landing, covered by another steel security shutter — which probably means it leads outside. Maybe you could break through the shutter with the fire axe. Or maybe you should keep running past the door, up the stairs towards the roof.

Kye hops down out of the vent. "Where are we going?" he asks. "They'll be right behind us!"

If you grab the fire axe and try to break through the security shutter, go to page 14.

If you take the stairs all the way up to the roof, go to page 26.

08:01

"**C**limb across," you say. "Quickly!"

"What?!" the man in the yellow shirt squeaks. "I'm not doing that!"

As the helicopter zooms closer, the wind picks up. The power cable sways from side to side over the deadly drop.

"We're sitting ducks up here," you say. "I'll hold it steady."

You grab the cable. It doesn't shock you, but you can feel it vibrating slightly, like a silent hum. You pull it tight so it's easier to climb on.

Kye looks scared, but he trusts you and he doesn't want to stand here arguing. He hangs underneath the cable and loops his legs over it, then he wiggles out over the street like an upside-down caterpillar.

Someone screams below. A woman behind the police barricade has spotted Kye. The police follow her gaze and start yelling at one another.

No time to wait for them to get their act together. The helicopter is nearly here.

You tug the cable. It feels steady enough to take more weight. "Who's next?" you ask.

The middle-aged woman with the fluffy scarf steps

forward. "I'll go." She takes hold of the cable and climbs out over the street.

Kye has almost reached the warehouse on the other side. He grabs the gutter, hauls himself up onto the metal roof and pumps his fist in the air.

"Wooo!" he cries. "I did it!"

The people behind the barricade cheer. The news cameras swing towards the woman with the scarf, who's halfway across. The other woman climbs onto the cable behind her.

"Hold it steady," you shout to Kye.

He does. With the cable anchored at both ends, the two women can crawl across even faster. The woman with the scarf has reached the warehouse.

"Now you," you tell the man in the yellow shirt. "Quickly!"

He reluctantly grabs the cable. He's heavier than anyone who has crossed so far. You struggle to hold the cable steady as he crosses his legs over it and pulls his way out over the void.

The helicopter thunders closer to the rooftop, tilted forward for speed. Now that it's closer, you can see the police colours on the side. There was no need to climb the cable after all. Help has arrived.

The man in the yellow shirt reaches the warehouse. You wave at the helicopter with both hands. "Hey! Down here!"

The stairwell door bursts open behind you. You whirl around. Miss Scarlet stands in the doorway, holding her laser. Her eyes glow with fury.

The cops won't be here in time to save you. So you leap onto the cable like a tightrope walker and sprint over the deadly drop.

The cable jerks violently beneath your shoes. The chopped air batters your head as the police helicopter sweeps past. You run towards Kye and the other three hostages, fighting to keep your balance.

A laser beam zips over your head, close enough that you feel the heat. You duck, but this leaves you looking down. The distant street wobbles beneath you.

But you're almost at the warehouse rooftop. Five more steps and you'll be there. Kye stretches out his hand for you to grab.

Zap! Another laser beam passes near your ankles. It misses you—

But it shears through the cable, cutting it off from the warehouse. The cable goes slack beneath your feet. You're falling!

If you leap towards the warehouse — and Kye's outstretched hand — go to page 29.

If you grab hold of the falling cable instead, go to page 32.

13:51

You scramble forwards, rushing at the man with the silver tooth as fast as you can. Startled, he drops the phone.

You grab for it. But he's too quick. He grips your shoulder with one hand and twists sideways, pinning you to the wall of the vent. His other hand clamps over your mouth.

"Shhh," he whispers. "I'm on your side."

You stare at him.

"I'm a cop," he says. "I've been undercover for months."

He releases you and opens a hidden pocket in his shirt sleeve. He pulls out a laminated card with a photograph of himself. It says: *Omar Alhamed, Detective.*

"This is no ordinary bank," Alhamed says. "The second floor is actually a secret laboratory. They're building experimental nanobots — millions of tiny machines, too small to see, designed to eat waste and turn it into more useful materials."

"That sounds like a crazy conspiracy theory," you say.

"That's what we thought too. Then we found some. Total fluke — a few bots somehow got flushed down a drain. Maybe a lab worker washed their hands at the wrong time. Anyway, the nanobots showed up in a water quality study near here. Believe me, they're real. That's why the robbers are here."

"Are the nanobots worth a lot of money?" you ask.

"They can be programmed to build almost anything. The robbers are going to program them to make a bomb."

"A bomb? Did you say bomb?" Your voice goes a bit squeaky.

"This way," Alhamed says and wiggles away backwards along the vent. You follow.

"What's happening up there?" whispers Kye, who has been stuck around the other side of the corner this whole time.

"One of the robbers is secretly a police officer," you whisper back. "He's taking us . . . somewhere."

Alhamed has reached another grill. He kicks it open and climbs down a ladder.

"The police should be outside by now," he says. "They can cut the power to stop the robbers from programming the nanobots. Then they can pump knock-out gas into the building through the air conditioning. But they won't do either of those things while the hostages are still in danger."

If you ask Alhamed how to get outside before that happens, turn to page 40.

If you ask him about the bomb instead, go to page 36.

12:09

You haul a wooden pallet underneath the air vent so the other hostages have something to land on.

"We'll head for the roof," you tell Kye. "There might be a fire escape. Or maybe we can barricade ourselves up there and get the attention of someone going past."

He nods. "Good idea."

The last of the hostages — a man in a pale yellow shirt — drops down onto the pallet.

"Why are we following a kid?" he asks the other hostages.

You open your mouth to defend yourself, but Kye gets there first.

"I don't see anyone else stepping up," he says. "Stay here if you want."

He starts running up the stairs and so do you. After a moment's hesitation, the other three hostages follow.

Only the first door is shuttered. The others you pass on the way up are accessible — but you ignore them. They probably lead to offices on the second, third and fourth floors. Somewhere to hide, maybe, but not to escape.

Still, it might help to let the robbers think you went that way. You shove one of the doors open as you run past. A fire alarm wails.

By the time you get to the top floor of the building, your thighs are burning and your lungs hurt. There's one last door, marked *ROOFTOP: UNAUTHORIZED ACCESS PROHIBITED.*

You push the door open and the sunrise blinds you. Stepping outside, you can see the roof is flat concrete, with a pit for a massive air-circulation machine and a platform for a radio antenna.

You run over to the edge of the rooftop and look down. Cops have sealed off both ends of the street. News crews stand behind the barricades.

"Hey!" You wave your arms. "Up here!"

They're too far away to hear you and all eyes are focused on the ground floor of the bank.

You throw your phone at them. It lands in a tree. No one notices.

The robbers will be up here any second. You look around desperately. There's no external fire escape. No way down.

A power cable connects this building to the warehouse across the street. It looks thick enough to take your weight. But is it electrified?

A distant sound grows nearer. *Thupthupthupthup.* You shade your eyes with one hand and see a helicopter racing towards the rooftop.

You're saved!

Unless this is the getaway helicopter for the robbers.

If it is, the pilot won't be pleased to see five escaped hostages. You'll have to get off this rooftop as fast as possible.

The other hostages are looking in your direction. You got them this far. They want your leadership.

If you tell them to climb across the power cable, go to page 21.

If you wait for the helicopter, go to page 30.

02:57

You're almost at the rooftop. Barely a metre away. It should be an easy jump. You leap towards the warehouse—

But you have nothing to jump off. The severed cable is slack, so your feet just push it away. You hurtle through the air on leftover momentum, arms windmilling, legs kicking.

Kye flings out a hand, trying to catch you before you fall. You reach for him, stretching every joint and tendon in your arm and shoulder.

Success! Kye grabs your hand. He tries to haul you up onto the warehouse rooftop—

But you're too heavy. He overbalances.

One of the other hostages tries to grab the back of Kye's shirt, but she's too slow. Kye topples off the roof and you both scream as you plummet down, down, down, accelerating towards the concrete below—

WHUMP!

THE END.

To try again, go back to page 26.

`08:01`

You wave to the helicopter as it thunders closer.

"Hey!" you yell, even though they can't possibly hear you. "Down here!"

The helicopter tilts and accelerates towards the rooftop. The wind from the blades nearly blasts you off your feet. But you can make out the word painted on the side — *POLICE*.

You were right!

The landing skids aren't even on the ground yet when the side door opens. A police officer in padded armour beckons. "Get in!" she yells.

The hostages run over and start climbing on board. They all keep their heads low, wary of the spinning blades above.

"Come on," Kye says, running over to the helicopter and jumping inside.

You're about to follow him when the stairwell door bursts open behind you. You turn to see Miss Scarlet and her laser framed in the doorway. Rage crackles in her eyes.

She takes aim at the helicopter.

You start to run, heart thudding.

Zap! A streak of light burns a scar along the side of

the helicopter. The reflected laser scorches the rooftop. It doesn't seem to penetrate the hull, but the pilot panics. The landing skids lurch upwards.

The helicopter is leaving. In seconds it'll be out of reach, leaving you alone on the rooftop with Miss Scarlet.

If you run and jump towards the helicopter, trying to catch the skids before it's out of reach, turn to page 34.

If you tackle Miss Scarlet and try to get the laser, turn to page 39.

02:57

s you plummet towards the concrete far below, you reach for the power cable with both hands. The torn end is spitting sparks.

Your left hand misses the cable. People are screaming down below. Cops are yelling.

Your right hand catches the cable.

The cable is still attached to the rooftop of the bank, so you swing back across the street like Tarzan on a vine. The air rushes past you, faster and faster. Squinting against the wind, you realize you're about to swing right into a second-storey window.

You let go, hoping to fall safely to the ground. Instead, you hit the window, shoes first.

Smash! You hurtle through the window and slide along the tiled floor in a puddle of broken glass.

"Ow," you groan.

Someone looms over you. He — or she, it's impossible to tell — is covered from head to toe in a white plastic suit. A mirrored visor reflects your own shock back at you.

Looking around, you see other workers in similar outfits, all staring at you. Giant machines dangle from the ceiling. Workbenches are littered with devices you don't recognize. This doesn't look like a bank.

A voice echoes over a loudspeaker. "OK, people. The police helicopter has landed on the roof and the robbers have been arrested. Show's over — everyone back to work."

The white-suited workers turn back to their benches and start looking through microscopes and fiddling with things too small for you to see.

"What is this place?" you ask.

The man with the mirrored visor jabs a finger at you. "You were never here and you never saw any of this. Got that?"

You nod dumbly.

"All right." He pulls you to your feet. "Let's get you out of here."

00:00

You survived! There are thirteen other ways to escape the danger — try to find them all!

03:20

You sprint towards the helicopter, hoping to grab the skids before it escapes into the sky. Your feet scuffle on the concrete rooftop.

Zap!

This time, Miss Scarlet isn't shooting at the helicopter. She's aiming at you. A laser beam sizzles over your head.

But you're almost there. Ten more steps.

Seven.

Your heart is pounding in your ears.

Four.

As the helicopter lurches higher up into the air, Miss Scarlet shoots again. The laser bolt narrowly misses your ear—

And melts through the glass of the cockpit.

The pilot rips his hands off the controls as the laser burns his fingers. The helicopter swings out of control. The passengers inside scream.

You leap forward to grasp the landing skids, but suddenly they're not there anymore. The helicopter has turned and tilted . . .

You're flying towards the spinning blades instead.

"Noooo!" you shriek.

But there's nothing to grab on to. No way to stop. You hurtle into the whirling helicopter blades and—

SPLAT!

THE END.

To try again, go back to page 26.

10:03

"**W**hat kind of device are they making?" you ask, as you climb down the ladder after Alhamed. The rungs chime like bells under your feet. "How far away do we have to get?"

"We can't get away from it," Alhamed says. "We can only stop it from going off."

You find yourself in a dimly lit maintenance room. Hammers and screwdrivers hang from rusty hooks. A mop is propped up in the corner next to an empty bucket. A first aid kit sits on a workbench next to someone's cellphone.

"The robbers came from a compound up in the mountains," Alhamed explains. "It started out as an environmentalist commune — carbon neutral, no modern tech, growing their own food and so on. But a few of them got together and came up with a more effective plan to protect the planet."

"What plan?"

"Get rid of all the people."

Your mouth goes dry. "How?"

Alhamed is unlocking a steel hatch in the corner of the floor. A stamp on the lid reads *CAUTION: SEWER*. He lifts the lid.

A foul smell fills the room. It's as though a dozen dogs have all farted at once.

"It's called a battery bomb," Alhamed says, and for a moment you think he's talking about the smell. "It broadcasts a signal to cellphones making them explode. But something like that is very hard to build. That's why they need the nanobots."

"Wait," you say. "They're trying to save the world by destroying the world?"

"Don't try to make sense of it," Alhamed says. "It's not rational. People like this never have a good reason to do what they do. It only ever fits together in their own heads."

He sounds gloomy. His months undercover with the robbers must have been tough.

The other hostages have climbed out of the vent into the maintenance room. Alhamed gestures to the hatch. "That's our way out," he tells them. "Grab the flashlight and the first aid kit."

Kye picks up the first aid kit. You take the flashlight off the workbench and hook it to your belt. Then you clamber through the hatch and climb down another ladder into the darkness of the sewer. The rungs are slippery. You're already starting to get used to the smell, but you're worried about diseases. Don't sewage treatment workers wear masks and gloves, to stop deadly bacteria from getting into their bodies?

You step off the ladder, only to discover that the ground isn't solid. *Splash!* You're standing knee-deep in foul-smelling water.

Kye climbs down the ladder after you. "Worst day ever," he grunts.

You're about to agree when someone screams in the maintenance room above.

"Down!" Alhamed roars. Then he kicks the hatch closed, separating you and Kye from the rest of the group.

The water laps quietly against the walls of the tunnel.

"What do we do now?" Kye whispers.

If you run up the sewer tunnel to find a way out and get help, go to page 44.

If you wait a minute and then try to sneak back through the hatch to help the others, go to page 49.

03:20

"**Y**aaargh!" Bellowing like a tenth-century warrior, you sprint towards Miss Scarlet.

Her eyes widen in astonishment. It takes her a second to recover — a second too long. You're already throwing yourself at her.

Wham! You knock Miss Scarlet off her feet and both of you hit the concrete, hard. It's not like tackling someone on the football field — every part of you hurts.

The laser goes flying. It lands on the rooftop a couple of metres away. Just out of reach.

"You've ruined everything!" Miss Scarlet screams.

Still on the ground, she lashes out at you. You raise your arm just in time to protect your face.

She's an experienced criminal. You're just a kid. Can you really hold her off until the cops get here?

Maybe — if you had the laser.

If you reach for the weapon, go to page 43.

If you try to hold Miss Scarlet down, go to page 47.

10:03

"How are we going to get out of the building?" you ask, climbing down the ladder after Alhamed.

You find yourself in a gloomy maintenance room. Wrenches and screwdrivers dangle from grimy hooks. A withered mop leans in the corner next to an empty bucket. A forgotten cellphone sits on a wooden bench beside a first aid kit.

"You're not going to like it," Alhamed says.

He is unlocking a steel hatch in the corner of the floor. A stamp on the lid reads *CAUTION: SEWER*.

"You're kidding," you say.

Alhamed lifts the lid. A foul smell washes over you. It's like visiting the dump on a forty-degree day.

You cover your mouth and nose. "There must be another way out."

Alhamed shrugs. "You could stay here with the robbers," he suggests. "But I wouldn't, if I were you."

"Why not?" you ask.

"You might survive until they turn on the device," Alhamed says.

"You mean the bomb?"

"Well, it's not exactly a bomb. It will send a signal to make all cellphone batteries explode. *They're* the bomb.

You probably don't want to stick around for that."

He must be kidding.

"But . . . *everyone* has a cellphone!" you exclaim.

"Exactly. We have to stop them. But the cops won't cut the power to the building until they know we're safe."

Kye is climbing down the ladder. "What is that smell?" he demands.

"That's your way out. Grab the first aid kit. And you" — Alhamed points at you — "get the flashlight. We'll need it."

You pick up the flashlight off the workbench and hook it into your belt. Kye snatches up the first aid kit.

The other hostages are climbing out of the vent into the maintenance room. Alhamed gestures to the hatch. "In you get."

Grumbling, you clamber down another slippery ladder into the foul-smelling shadows. You try not to breathe.

You step off the ladder and splash into stinky, knee-deep water. Mysterious blobs float past.

You can't wait to get home and take a long, hot shower.

Kye climbs down after you. "Smells like my brother's room," he grunts.

You're trying not to laugh when a scream rings out from above.

"Down!" Alhamed roars. Then he kicks the hatch closed.

You and Kye are now on your own in the sewer, with no idea what's happening up in the maintenance room.

The water gurgles and swirls around your legs. Slime drips from the walls of the tunnel.

"What now?" Kye hisses.

If you run up the sewer tunnel so you can find a way out and get help, go to page 44.

If you wait a minute and then try to sneak back through the hatch to help the others, go to page 49.

02:13

You let go of Miss Scarlet, scramble to your feet and run to the fallen laser. It's only a few steps away.

Miss Scarlet doesn't chase you. She doesn't even get up.

You snatch up the laser. It's surprisingly heavy. The grip is cold against your palm. You're not sure how to fire it, but that doesn't matter. It's just supposed to be a threat.

You whirl around to face Miss Scarlet and raise the weapon. "Stay back!"

She still hasn't gotten up, but she's pulled an object out of the pouch at her waist. It's hard to tell, but it looks like some kind of miniature remote control — the kind people use to unlock their cars or open their garages.

"Game over," she tells you.

Then she pushes the button.

The laser beeps in your hands.

You look down. The grip is becoming uncomfortably hot. The metal glows. You drop it and turn to run, but—

KABOOM!

THE END.
To try again, go back to page 30.

07:02

"**W**e need to get out of here and find the police," you tell Kye. "Come on."

You slosh up the tunnel, away from the ladder. Kye follows you.

It's too dark to see anything. You flick on the flashlight and sweep it across the tunnel as you walk. The walls are encrusted with old gunk. The water has a strange silvery sheen.

"Is that another hatch?" Kye asks, pointing ahead.

You raise the flashlight and squint into the distance. There is something on the ceiling, but it's too far away to be sure what it is.

"Maybe," you say. "Let's go."

You wade through the water, grimacing. At least it's not cold. The bacteria must keep it warm, like compost. Gross.

"Ow!"

You turn around. Kye is clutching his leg.

"What happened?" you ask.

"It's like . . . something bit me. And it's still biting me. Ow, ow!"

You run back to Kye. He pulls up his pant leg. There's nothing on him.

You scan the dark water. It never occurred to you that something might be living down here. Leeches? Piranhas? Baby crocodiles, flushed down someone's toilet?

"It hurts!" Kye moans. The skin of his leg turns pink, then red — like an ugly rash.

Suddenly you can feel it too. A stinging pain in your shins, as though you've walked into the tentacles of a jellyfish. When you look down, you see holes in your pants — and the holes are getting wider. You rub your legs, trying to brush off whatever is attacking you. The palms of your hands start to sting and turn pink.

"Run!" you scream, although you're not even sure what you're running from. You both splash through the waste to what you desperately hope is another hatch—

The waste.

. . . designed to eat waste and turn it into more useful materials . . . a few bots somehow got flushed down a drain . . .

You shine the light on your throbbing hand. A sandy grey substance is stuck to your palm. When you look closely, you can see the tiny grains moving on their own.

"The escaped nanobots!" you yell. "They're eating us!"

"The what?!" Kye sounds like he thinks you're losing your mind. But you're sure you're right. Alhamed said that some of the escaped nanobots had showed up in a water quality study, but he didn't say that *all* of them had been found. If they could build anything, maybe they could multiply by building copies of themselves.

Your skin is bright red and blotchy. Will the nanobots realize you're not garbage and stop eating?

You stick your hand in the water and splash it around, trying to wash the nanobots off. It doesn't work. They hang on tightly with their tiny jaws.

"Fire!" Kye says. He pulls a box of matches out of the first aid kit. "We can burn them off!"

Getting burned might be better than being eaten alive, but it will hurt. Maybe there's another way.

Batteries can cause an electric shock. Instead of matches, perhaps you can use the battery in your phone to short-circuit the nanobots somehow.

If you strike a match, turn to page 51.

If you start disassembling your phone, turn to page 54.

02:13

Miss Scarlet crawls across the concrete towards the fallen laser, but you grab her legs. She kicks at you with her heavy boots. A sharp pain in your chest makes it hard to breathe. Gritting your teeth, you hang on to her legs.

She rolls over, pulling her feet free. Then she clambers towards you and puts her hand on your throat. Your vision goes blurry. She's choking you.

A cold wind washes over your body. Is this what passing out feels like?

But no.

It's the helicopter, sweeping over the top of you.

"What the—" Miss Scarlet doesn't get any farther. A dangling hook has caught the hood of her jacket. She screams, terrified, as the helicopter lifts her up into the air. It's like watching an angler pull a wiggling fish out of the water.

You can breathe again! You roll over, coughing, as the helicopter swings out over the street. Miss Scarlet has grabbed the hook and is holding on tight trying not to fall.

You drag yourself over to the edge of the rooftop and look down. Police officers swarm all over the street below, waiting for the helicopter to lower Miss Scarlet down.

You rest your head on the cold concrete of the rooftop. It's over.

00:00

You survived! There are thirteen other ways to escape the danger — try to find them all!

07:02

You make a shushing gesture at Kye and then climb slowly and carefully back up the ladder.

You listen from beneath the hatch.

Silence.

You're not sure what just happened up above. Maybe one of the robbers came into the maintenance room, saw the escaping hostages and attacked them. If so, there's probably nothing you can do. There are no voices above.

But you can't just leave them behind.

So you wait. Long enough for the robbers to decide they've dealt with the problem. Long enough for them to escort any surviving hostages out of the room.

Long enough to notice that two kids are missing.

The hatch lifts up above your head, bathing you in light. You yelp and try to scramble down the ladder, but you're too slow. Mr. Sharp — the man with the knife tattoo — grabs you by the collar and hauls you out of the hatch. He dumps you on the floor of the maintenance room, next to Alhamed and the other three hostages. All four are unconscious. Mr. Sharp grips the laser.

"Run, Kye!" you scream.

There's a series of splashes from below. Kye is fleeing up the sewer tunnel towards safety.

Mr. Sharp curses. He doesn't want to leave you alone, but he can't let Kye get away. He looks down at the hatch, as though preparing to jump.

If you try to stop him, he'll have plenty of time to zap you with the laser. But if you don't, he'll drop down into the sewer and blast Kye instead.

If you attack Mr. Sharp with the flashlight, go to page 52.

If you do nothing and let him climb down into the sewer, go to page 57.

04:19

Kye tosses the matchbox to you. Good decision — he's hopeless with matches. At his brother's birthday party, it took him several minutes to light all the candles. You don't have that kind of time right now.

You dig out a match. Your hands sting. Your legs are in agony still standing in the sewage. Even if you do manage to burn up all the nanobots, you still might die of infection.

With a trembling hand, you strike the match. No spark.

"Hurry!" Kye urges.

You strike the match again.

A spark lights up—

KABOOM!

The methane — the horrible-smelling gas in the air — ignites. A fireball explodes outwards from the matchbox—

Go to page 123.

04:19

You scramble to your feet and charge at Mr. Sharp, brandishing the flashlight.

He points the laser at you and pulls the trigger.

Zap!

A bolt of lightning hits you square in the chest.

It tickles. That's it.

You're so surprised that you miss a step and almost trip over. The laser must be running out of batteries. The charge is so low that it doesn't even hurt.

You lunge at Mr. Sharp, swinging the flashlight—

But he snatches the flashlight out of your hand and swats you out of the air like a fly. You hit the ground.

"Urgh." You roll over, joints aching.

Mr. Sharp raises the flashlight, about to bring it crashing down onto you . . .

And then he sneezes.

You stare at him. He sneezes again, blinking furiously. His eyes are watering. He staggers sideways, losing his balance. Then he falls face first onto the concrete floor.

What just happened? You sit up and suddenly you're dizzy too. A strange smell lingers in the air, like burning oil. Your ears are ringing.

Alhamed's voice echoes through your head.

. . . they can pump knock-out gas into the building through the air conditioning.

The police must have arrived. You can hear stern, authoritative voices echoing from other parts of the building. You pull your T-shirt over your nose, trying to filter out the gas.

"Down here!" you try to shout. But only the "Down—" comes out before you slump sideways onto the floor, asleep.

00:00

You survived! There are thirteen other ways to escape the danger — try to find them all!

04:19

"**W**e can electrify them!" you yell, and you dig your phone out of your pocket.

"No, burn them!" Kye prods you with the matches, as though you simply didn't hear him the first time.

You ignore him as you rip open your phone case. You can't just poke the nanobots with the battery. That might shock one or two of them, maybe. But there would still be millions of nanobots ripping at your skin.

"On the count of three," you say, "I want you to duck under the water."

Kye looks aghast. The water is foul. "Under it?"

"Trust me," you say, although you're not sure this will work. "One." You pull the batteries out of the flashlight as well. "Two," you say.

Kye looks torn. He's probably wondering whether being eaten alive would be better than diving under sewer water.

The nanobots have spread to your knees and wrists. The pain is unbearable.

"Three!" you yell. Then you throw the handful of batteries into the air and dive down into the water.

The world goes quiet and dark. You keep your eyes and mouth tightly closed.

The batteries hit the water above your head with a sequence of muffled splashes. You don't hear them discharge, but you feel the electric shock zap through the water — a sudden but slight tingling in your scalp and your fingertips.

You stand back up, gasping for air. Kye is already up, spluttering and gagging.

"Did it work?" he gasps.

You look down at your hand. It still hurts, but the nanobots are gone. Hopefully they released their jaws when they got electrified. Hopefully.

"I think so," you say. "But I can't see. I need light."

Both of you wade over to a nearby ladder. The thing above is a hatch — or a manhole cover, at least.

You climb the ladder and push upwards. But the cover is too heavy.

"Help me," you grunt.

Kye climbs up beside you. Shoulder to shoulder, you both heave upwards, shoving the manhole cover out of its slot.

You clamber through the gap into the early morning light. You're smeared with muck and your clothes are ripped all over. You must look like a zombie climbing out of a grave. But no one sees you. The street is deserted. Dust, or maybe ash, blows past you in the breeze.

Kye hauls himself out of the manhole. "I have never needed a bath so badly," he grumbles.

"Yeah." You examine your skin. Almost all the nano-bots are gone. You shake loose the remaining ones and they fall right off. You're safe.

"We have to call the police," you say.

Kye digs out his phone and tries to turn it on. Eventually he gives up. "The water broke my phone," he says. "Where is everyone?"

Good question. There are no pedestrians. No traffic noise. All the cars are parked in the middle of the street, empty.

"We need a phone." Kye opens a car door. It's unlocked. A pile of ash spills out onto the road. A blackened phone lands on top of the pile.

You suddenly feel dizzy. As you stumble, you see the street again — lots of ash. No people.

"The device," you whisper.

"The what?" Kye asks.

You fall, landing on your backside. It's too late to call the police. No one will answer. Everyone with a phone is a goner. If you hadn't ruined your phone batteries in the sewer, you would be too.

It's just you and Kye in a quiet, empty world.

00:00

You survived! There are thirteen other ways to escape the danger — try to find them all!

04:19

You keep your hands raised and wait for Mr. Sharp to climb down into the sewer.

But he doesn't. He leaves the hatch open and runs over to the workbench. He grabs a hammer and spins it in his hand.

"What are you—"

He doesn't let you finish the sentence. He swings the hammer.

You duck. The hammer swooshes by your head.

You scramble past him, but there's nowhere to go. You're trapped between him and the workbench.

"I surrender," you yell, holding up your hands. "You win!"

After a long moment, Mr. Sharp lowers the hammer.

You exhale slowly.

Then Mr. Sharp spots something on the workbench behind you. Something that terrifies him.

"No," he whispers. "No!"

You turn to look, but there's nothing scary on the bench. Just the cellphone you saw earlier.

Mr. Sharp dives down the hatch into the sewer. Not chasing Kye, but running for his life.

You remember what Alhamed said about the device

the robbers were building. The device that they would switch on, as soon as it was ready.

The phone beeps.

You turn to run—

Flash! A shockwave blasts outwards from the phone and turns you to dust.

THE END.

Go back to page 24 to try again!

15:15

The phone starts ringing. A *bleep-bleep* sound, like an old-fashioned video game.

"You're on, kid," Miss Scarlet says, pointing to the phone.

You hesitate. "You don't need to hurt anyone," you say. "I'm sure the police will give you whatever you want."

Miss Scarlet waves the laser towards you. That seems to be her response to any sort of disagreement. "Answer the phone right now."

You pick up the phone. "Hello?"

"Hi. My name's Jess. Can I ask who I'm speaking with?"

She doesn't sound like a police officer. You tell her your name.

"OK," Jess says. "My first question to you is, are you OK? Have you been injured?"

"No," you say.

"What about the other people in the building?" Her voice is careful. "Does anyone need medical attention?"

"I don't think so," you say.

Miss Scarlet is getting impatient. "Code," she says. "Now."

"We need the code to unlock the vault," you say.

"We have hostages," Miss Scarlet adds.

"She has hostages," you say.

"Who is 'she'?" Jess asks. "Maybe I should speak with her."

You look at Miss Scarlet, who shakes her head.

"No," you say. "Sorry."

"I really need to talk to the person in charge," Jess says. "Otherwise I can't do anything for you."

If you tell her you're a hostage and that the robbers refuse to talk, go to page 85.

If you tell her you're the one in charge, go to page 80.

10:41

iss Scarlet looks over just as you finish typing and step back. "Don't touch that," she says. "You have no idea how dangerous it is."

"I was just looking," you say.

A progress bar has appeared on the screen. It's already at two percent.

The building is rocked by another explosion. This time the noise comes from the other side — it sounds like the bank is under attack from several fronts. Hopefully the cops are rescuing the other hostages right now.

"We can't wait any longer!" Mr. Signet yells.

"Activate the nanobots!" Miss Scarlet says. "Start building the device!"

This sounds like nonsense to you, but Mr. Signet seems to know what she means. He runs over to the box and starts typing on the keypad.

Whatever he's trying to do, it isn't working. He looks more and more panicked. "They're not responding!"

"What?" Miss Scarlet whirls around. "Why not?"

"It's like they're already building something!"

"Well, stop them!"

Mr. Signet keeps typing. You can hear boots tromping through the building. The police are coming.

Miss Scarlet looks at you. "What did you do?" she snarls.

You try to look innocent.

She grabs your arms and pushes you against the wall.

"Tell me!" Spittle flecks your face.

If you tell her what you did to the box, go to page 64.

If you try to struggle free so you can run for the vault door, go to page 66.

05:09

"What was that?" Miss Scarlet asks.

Mr. Signet shrugs. Mr. Sharp is staring at the box.

There it is again: *thump, thump.*

Something is inside. But what?

"What did you do?" Miss Scarlet asks again.

Behind her, the lid of the box springs open. Fingers appear over the edge. A hand, pulling itself up.

Miss Scarlet turns to look at the box just in time to see a face emerge.

Your face. Somehow, the person in the box is you.

You scream. It's impossible not to. Seeing your own reflection — but not a reflection, a whole other being, an impossible twin — breaks your brain. This person has your eyes, your mouth, your hair. Somehow, typing in your own name created a perfect copy of you.

The other version of you screams as well. Miss Scarlet looks from you, to you and back again. Then she raises the laser towards the clone of you inside the box.

If you shout out a warning to the other you, go to page 65.

If you try to grab the laser, go to page 67.

07:36

"If you hurt me, you'll never get it open," you say.

You can hear Miss Scarlet's teeth grinding.

"I set a password," you continue. "You can't open it without my help."

Miss Scarlet looks at Mr. Signet. "Is that true?"

"No," he says. "I can get it open. We just have to wait for the current operation to finish."

"How long will that take?" she asks.

"Two minutes, tops."

"Any point keeping the kid alive?"

Mr. Signet looks at you, chewing his lip.

If you typed in your own name, go to page 72.

If you typed in something else, go to page 76.

`02:50`

"**W**atch out!" you yell. "Get back down!"

But you're too late. A laser blast hits the clone. The other you falls, disappearing back into the box.

"No!" you scream.

"We're out of time," Miss Scarlet tells the other robbers. "Grab some nanobots and go."

Mr. Sharp pulls a travel mug out of his bag and starts digging in the box.

"What about the kid?" Mr. Signet asks.

You lunge for the exit—

But Mr. Signet trips you.

You hit the concrete floor. The world is spinning.

"No witnesses," Miss Scarlet says.

Something strikes you and the whole world goes dark.

THE END.

Return to page 137 to try again!

07:36

You try to pry Miss Scarlet's hands off your arms so you can run out of the vault. But she's too strong. Then there's a third *kaboom* from somewhere else in the building. Miss Scarlet loses her balance. Her hands loosen for a split second. You slip free, hit the floor and sprint towards the vault door. Mr. Signet tries to tackle you. He misses and crash-lands on the concrete.

A laser beam shoots past you as you dash through the open door. Miss Scarlet is trying to fry you, but her aim is off. You're almost at the staff door that leads back into the main part of the bank. You're going to make it.

But a huge hand grabs your collar. Mr. Sharp drags you backwards. He's unbelievably strong.

"No!" you yell. "Get off me!"

You may as well be pleading with a robot. He hauls you, kicking and squirming, back to the vault.

Then you hear a noise from inside the box.

If you typed in your own name, go to page 63.

If you typed in RHINOCEROS, go to page 73.

If you typed in BEEHIVE, go to page 69.

02:50

You grab Miss Scarlet's weapon, just in time. The laser beam misses your clone and carves a line through the concrete wall instead.

But the barrel of the laser burns your hand. You let go, stung.

Miss Scarlet tries to fire again, but the weapon clicks empty.

The battery is dead.

She raises a fist—

And then your clone crash-tackles her. They both hit the floor, hard.

Not knowing the laser is dead, your clone tries to grab it. Miss Scarlet takes the opportunity to flip the other you off her. She pins the clone to the floor—

But a dozen police officers swarm through the open vault door. Finally. Shouts fill the air as two of the officers pull Miss Scarlet off your clone and handcuff her. Others grab Mr. Sharp and Mr. Signet, who don't put up much of a fight. They're still stunned from seeing a copy of you climb out of the box.

Miss Scarlet thrashes like an electric eel, but the cops holding her are too strong.

You hold out a hand and help your clone to stand up.

The two of you stare at one another for a long time.

"What do we do now?" you both say, at the same moment.

00:00

You survived! There are thirteen other ways to escape the danger—try to find them all!

05:09

A sinister hum emanates from the box. It sounds like an enormous amount of power is being routed through it.

"What's going on?" Miss Scarlet asks Mr. Signet. "Is it fixed?"

"I don't know," Mr. Signet says. He leans over the box.

The progress bar reaches 100 percent.

With a *ding* like an oven timer, the lid of the box launches itself open. From where you are standing, you can't see inside—but you can see the look on the robbers' faces. They recoil in shock.

A glittering golden cloud rises from the box. The humming gets louder and you realize it's not electrical. It's coming from millions and millions of bees.

Somehow, when you typed the word *BEEHIVE* into the keypad, the box started making an actual beehive and filling it with actual bees. It seems impossible — like magic — but it's true.

"Get them off me!" Mr. Signet says. He's slapping at his arms as though he's on fire.

"Stop!" Miss Scarlet yells. "You're making them aggressive!"

Mr. Signet doesn't stop. He keeps flailing like a

lunatic. Red welts appear all over his face as the bees sting him. His hands swell up like red sponges.

Now that he's made them angry, the bees turn on Miss Scarlet. You remember reading somewhere that bee stings release pheromones that encourage other bees to attack. Miss Scarlet screams as the insects sting her neck and arms. She tears at her hair, trying to get them off her scalp, but there are too many.

And still more are flooding from the open box. The edge of the swarm draws nearer.

A stunned Mr. Sharp has loosened his grip. You shake off his hand and run away from the vault, back the way you came. He chases you — or maybe he's just fleeing from the bees. The humming is deafening now.

Something lands on your hair, buzzing. You swat it away as you run. Something else joins it. There's a sudden sharp pain behind your ear. The flesh around the sting grows hot.

"Ow!" You keep running, with increasing panic. Another sting punctures the nape of your neck. Bees have crawled up your shirt cuffs and are buzzing around inside your clothes.

The pain is unbearable. You're getting dizzy.

"Help me," you gasp, but you're barely sure who you're talking to. You're not even sure the words come out. Your eyelids are swelling up. You can't see.

You hit the floor.

The last thing you hear is humming and buzzing, humming and buzzing.

THE END.

Return to page 137 to try again.

06:05

"Not in my opinion," Mr. Signet says finally.

"Wait," you say. "He's lying. I can get it open!"

"No," Mr. Signet says. "Nothing we can do but wait for it to finish."

Miss Scarlet points the laser at you.

"No!" you shriek. "Stop!"

She pulls the trigger.

There's a bright flash and then the whole world disappears.

WHOOSH!

Go to page 77.

05:09

There's a horrible groan from inside the box. Like the creaking of a ship, or maybe the cracking of a sheet of ice. Something is bending and breaking.

Without warning, the box explodes like an egg in a microwave. Sharp pieces of metal shower the vault, clanging into the corners.

Standing where the box used to be is a rhinoceros.

You stumble backwards. You can't believe it.

The rhinoceros is impossibly huge in the vault and it's growing as you watch. Black eyes stare at you from leathery sockets. Huge feet scuff the base of the shattered box. A massive horn sways left and right, as though deciding who to skewer first.

Too late, you realize what the box was — a device that could make anything. The robbers wanted it to make what they called a "battery bomb." But when you typed in the word *RHINOCEROS*, you summoned this gigantic beast instead.

The rhino snorts, furious to discover itself trapped in this room. It turns to face you, puts its head down and charges.

You can't get out of the way. Mr. Sharp is still holding your shirt. You scream as two tonnes of animal flesh hurtles towards you. The point of the deadly horn is heading right for you.

Then Miss Scarlet fires the laser.

She probably wasn't trying to save you. The rhino is between her and the vault door — she probably wanted to hurt it so she could escape. But when the laser beam rakes across that tough skin, the rhino roars and changes direction. Suddenly it is stampeding towards Miss Scarlet, horn first.

You can't watch. You cover your eyes. There's a mighty crash and the sound of receding hooves.

Dust pours down on your head. Coughing, you open your eyes. Half of one wall is missing. A cool breeze sweeps in from outside. Miss Scarlet and the rhino are nowhere to be seen.

Mr. Sharp lets go of you, stunned. You almost fall over. It's like your legs have forgotten how to hold you up.

Sirens fill the air, covering the distant thunder of the rhino's hooves.

"We gotta go," Mr. Signet says to Mr. Sharp. "Come on, man! Run!"

He runs through the hole in the wall, but is immediately grabbed by a man in SWAT gear. Police are flooding into the room, checking corners with flashlights and shouting to each other. Two of them grab Mr. Sharp and wrestle him to the ground.

One of them holds a gloved hand out to you.

"You OK, kid?" he asks.

You just stare at the hole in the wall.

"What happened here?" the cop asks.

"I have no idea," you say.

00:00

You survived! There are thirteen other ways to escape the danger — try to find them all!

06:05

"I doubt it," Mr. Signet says at last. "But it's your call."

Miss Scarlet thinks for a moment. You wonder what's going on behind those evil eyes.

She points the laser at you.

"No!" you scream. "He can't open it! I can! I set a password!"

Ignoring you, Miss Scarlet pulls the trigger.

The universe flashes.

ZING!

THE END.

Return to page 137 to try again.

05:40

You wake up in absolute darkness, lying on a cold, hard surface. Your breaths reverberate around you, bouncing back immediately. You've been packed into a tight space.

A coffin. Someone must have thought you were dead — and now you've been buried alive!

You stifle a scream, not wanting to waste the oxygen. Maybe they didn't bury you that deep. Maybe you can dig your way out.

You can't lift your knees. The walls are tight on either side of your shoulders. But you can get your hands against the lid and push.

It pops right open. Fluorescent light floods in. You're not buried and this isn't a coffin. It's the box — the one you typed your name into. You're still in the vault.

Thoroughly confused, you climb out of the box. No sign of the robbers — but there's a body on the floor.

It's you.

Your knees go weak. You feel like you might throw up.

That isn't a copy, you realize. *You're* the copy. Somehow, when you typed in your name, the box started making a clone of you. And then the robbers zapped the original version.

Voices echo from outside the vault. The robbers, discussing what to do next.

A terrible fury floods through your body.

The nearest potential weapon is a fire extinguisher. You wrench it off the wall, barely noticing how heavy it is as you carry it out of the vault.

In the staff-only area, the three robbers are standing in a circle. Mr. Signet is talking about the police cordon and how to break through.

Miss Scarlet sees you first. The colour drains from her face. "What . . ." she whispers. "How . . ." She probably thinks you're a ghost. In a way, she's right.

The other robbers turn. Mr. Sharp screams like a little kid. You raise the fire extinguisher, ready to hurl it with all your might.

Mr. Signet snatches the laser off Miss Scarlet's belt and shoots. He misses you, but the energy bolt punches a hole through the extinguisher. A grey cloud of gas billows out of the hole.

You throw the extinguisher. It doesn't hit anyone, or at least, you don't think so. It vanishes into the mist and clangs to the floor somewhere beyond.

Still fuelled by rage, you storm towards where the robbers were standing. You lash out, but hit nothing. They must have gone into the customer area of the bank.

You fumble your way past the counter and through the staff-only door. The terrified robbers are fiddling with the shutter over the front door, trying to get it open.

"Hello," you say.

They whirl around and see you, looming a few steps behind them, arms hanging loose by your sides. Mr. Signet yelps. The other two claw at the door. You walk through the ankle-deep mist towards them as though you're floating.

Miss Scarlet finally manages to unlock the shutter. Mr. Sharp lifts it and they all sprint through the foyer, out into the light of dawn. The street is thick with police.

Desperate to get away from the vengeful ghost behind them, the robbers immediately surrender. They stick their hands up and run to the police cars. Mr. Signet yells, "Get us out of here!"

You stand in the doorway and watch the police take the robbers away.

00:00

You survived! There are thirteen other ways to escape the danger — try to find them all!

11:05

"I'm in charge," you say, trying to make your voice sound deeper. "And I'm telling you we want the code. Not later. Right now."

Miss Scarlet looks taken aback. Behind her, Mr. Signet is trying not to laugh. You can feel yourself getting tangled deeper and deeper in this mess.

"OK," Jess says. "I can make that happen. But first I need to know the hostages are OK."

"They're fine," you say.

"I need proof. Send one out the front door and they can verify that everything is OK inside."

Miss Scarlet shakes her head.

"We don't have time for that," you say. "Just give us the code and we'll be out of here. No one will get hurt."

You look at Miss Scarlet as you say this. It's like you're giving her an order. As though you really are in charge.

"I have one of the bank's employees with me," Jess says. "It's her day off. She says the vault code is written on a sticky note on the table closest to the vault door."

You look. There it is. You point it out to Miss Scarlet. She grabs it and runs over to the vault door.

"Now you have what you want," Jess continues. "So you can let the hostages go."

The vault door is now wide open. Mr. Signet and Mr. Sharp run inside. "Sure," you say.

Miss Scarlet shakes her head again.

"I mean, no," you say. "Not yet. But soon."

The two men come out of the vault dragging a metal box, about the size of a desk.

"Our getaway car is coming," Miss Scarlet whispers. "A black van. The police need to let it through."

"I need you to let a black van through the police cordon," you say. "We'll jump in and leave. Then you can come in and get the hostages."

"Except one," Miss Scarlet says and points at you. With a sinking feeling, you realize that the robbers are taking you with them.

"Don't shoot the van," you tell Jess. "There'll be a hostage inside."

Miss Scarlet mimes hanging up. You put the phone back on the hook.

"Good job, 'boss,'" she says. "Let's go."

You follow Miss Scarlet into the customer area of the bank. The two men carry the box out after you.

Do you grab a bundle of cash off the cart on your way out, or do you leave it? Make your choice and then turn to page 87 . . .

Unless you run back and lock yourself in the vault so the robbers can't get you, then go to page 90.

04:21

You run over to the steel box. The keypad doesn't seem to have a cancel button. The screen has a progress bar, which says: *11 . . . 12 . . . 13 . . . 14.*

You lift the lid. It's not locked. Inside, you can't see the nanobots, but you can see what they're making. You were expecting wires, a countdown timer and maybe a nice big *OFF* switch. Instead, there is just a pile of grey slush, getting bigger and bigger. You can't defuse this. It has no fuses.

Too late to run. You look around the room, desperate. No sign of the ninja. Maybe if you dump water on the slush the nanobots won't be able to ignite it. But there are no buckets, no taps, no water bottles.

You look at the vault. Thick concrete walls. A solid steel door. Maybe you don't need to stop the box from exploding. Maybe you just need to put it back where it came from.

You drag the box back towards the vault. It's heavy and seems to get heavier as the nanobots build more and more explosive slush — although that seems impossible, since they must be getting the materials from somewhere.

You haul the box into the vault and run out. Your

arms burning, you push the mighty steel door closed. The locks engage automatically.

Now you run. Out of the staff room and through the customer area. There's no sign of the other hostages. Someone has unlocked the shutters over the front doors. Maybe the ninja opened them on his way in, or perhaps Miss Scarlet did it on her way out.

You can almost feel the pile of explosive slush growing in the vault behind you, getting closer and closer to detonation.

The street is chaotic. Police are running around everywhere. Journalists and camera operators are fighting to get through a police cordon set up around the bank. The other hostages are wrapped in blankets, huddled next to ambulances. Miss Scarlet has been caught. She's on the ground, yelling furiously as the ninja binds her wrists together with glue.

"Run!" you scream. "There's a—"

BOOM!

A shockwave rolls out from the bank. You stagger and almost collapse. The windows blow out, showering the street with glass. Concrete crackles like fireworks. And then the building is falling, caving in on itself like a half-baked cake. A fog of dust chokes the street. Soon you can't see anything.

Eventually silence falls. Coughing, you pat yourself down. You're not hurt. People are shouting, but no one is screaming. You can't see anything, but it sounds like everyone is scared rather than injured. The vault contained the explosion.

"Kye!" you yell.

"I'm here," calls a voice in the distance.

Kye is covered in so much dust that he looks like a black-and-white photo. You run over and hug him.

"What happened to you?" he asks.

"Long story," you say.

00:00

You survived! There are thirteen other ways to escape the danger — try to find them all!

11:05

"I'm just a hostage," you say. "I can't make them talk to you."

Her tone becomes less soothing, for some reason. "OK. But I assume they can hear every word I'm saying, is that right?"

You look at Miss Scarlet for permission to admit that, but Jess keeps talking. "You and the other hostages just sit tight. Don't try to intervene. We'll get this resolved very soon."

The robbers don't seem very keen on negotiating. You wonder how Jess thinks the situation will be "resolved."

"The code," Miss Scarlet says.

"They want the code for the vault," you say.

"The bank's staff called us from the panic room," Jess says. "They say it's written on a sticky note on the table near the vault."

You look over. There it is. How did you miss that?

Miss Scarlet has already spotted it. "Great," she says. "That's all we need. Hang up."

You're reluctant. Jess is the only thread connecting you to the safe world outside.

"Now," Miss Scarlet says.

Jess says one last thing. Her voice is muffled, quiet. She's talking to someone else at the other end of the line.

"Send in the ninja," she says.

Wondering what that means, you hang up.

Mr. Signet and Mr. Sharp have opened the vault door. They're dragging a metal box out.

"Be careful with that," Miss Scarlet tells them. "We need it in perfect working order."

There's a *thump*.

"What did I just say?" she snaps.

"That wasn't us," Mr. Signet says.

They all look at you. You raise your hands. "I didn't do anything."

As the three robbers scan the room for the source of the mysterious thump, you notice a drip of water on the floor. You smudge it with your shoe and look up.

A man is stuck to the ceiling.

At least, you think it's a man. His baggy clothes cover everything except his eyes. The shiny fabric should make him stand out, but instead it makes him practically invisible — just a shimmer in the air. He looks right at you.

You turn back to the robbers. They haven't noticed him yet, but it can't be long before they look up too. You need to distract them.

If you ask what's in the box, go to page 93.

If you ask to go back to where the other hostages are, go to page 99.

09:12

You follow the robbers out into the waiting area. The hostages are still huddled up against the wall. Kye watches you walk past with frightened eyes.

"It's OK," you tell him. "The police are coming in soon."

"No talking," Miss Scarlet snaps.

Mr. Sharp and Mr. Signet drag the box into the airlock-style foyer and wait by the shuttered front door.

The city outside sounds unnaturally quiet. The police must have evacuated the area.

"Where's Omar?" Mr. Sharp asks. "How long does it take to sabotage an air conditioner?"

You'd completely forgotten the fourth robber — the man with the silver tooth and the overalls. Where has he been all this time?

"Forget him," Miss Scarlet says. "If he's not here when the van arrives, we're leaving him behind."

"He can identify us."

"That won't matter for long."

Tires screech outside.

"That's our ride," Miss Scarlet says. She unlocks the door.

Go to the next page.

08:29

The getaway van is the same one that sped past you less than thirty minutes ago, although it feels like a lifetime has passed since then. The side door is open. The driver is hidden in the shadows inside.

Plenty of cops are around, but they all keep their distance. It's as though you have a contagious disease. They stand behind cop cars and peer out from alleyways. Silhouettes, which might be police snipers, are visible atop nearby buildings. Even Mr. Sharp and Mr. Signet look nervous as they haul the box into the van.

Not Miss Scarlet, though. She scans her surroundings casually and says, "All right. Everybody in."

You clamber into the van. The inside smells like glass cleaner. The driver is a pot-bellied man with a huge moustache and bristly sideburns.

The robbers sit on the box in back of the van. Miss Scarlet makes you sit up the front next to the driver, where she can watch you but you can't easily see her. You buckle your seatbelt.

Miss Scarlet closes the door. "Get us out of here," she tells the driver.

The van lurches through a gap in the police cordon and zooms towards the highway.

"Where are you going to drop me off?" you ask.

There's silence. The van goes up a ramp and trundles onto a bridge across the river.

Right now, they need you alive. The cops are still close by, and only your presence is stopping them from attacking the van. Once the robbers have given them the slip, they won't need you anymore. But does that mean they'll let you go?

This could be your last chance to escape. Right now the van is driving pretty slowly. A crash would probably not be fatal.

If you grab the steering wheel and try to crash the van into a street-light, turn to page 91.

If you ask them to pull over so you can throw up, turn to page 95.

09:12

When the robbers aren't looking, you dash back towards the vault. You slip through the doorway and grab the steel door. It weighs a ton, but the hinges are well oiled. You haul it closed. It hits the frame with a boom and locks automatically.

You rub your hands together nervously. The vault seems airtight. You're not sure how much oxygen is in there. Hopefully enough to last until the cops come in to let you out.

A quiet sound reaches your ears. Something tapping, scratching, tapping. You look around the vault. Nothing is moving. The noise must be coming from outside.

The door clanks. Someone has unlocked it from the other side.

You back away as the door swings open, revealing the three robbers. Miss Scarlet looks amused. The other two just look annoyed.

"You gave us the code, remember?" Mr. Signet says.

"Well, a stupid hostage is a safe hostage." Miss Scarlet gestures with the laser. "Come on, kid."

You meekly follow them out of the vault.

Go to page 88.

05:16

You slowly and carefully unbuckle your seatbelt. The robbers don't notice you moving, but Miss Scarlet hears the click.

"What was that?" She looks around.

You don't give her time to figure it out. You lunge forward and grab the steering wheel.

The driver curses. He snatches the wheel back and shoves you away. You flop sideways, winded.

The van is about to hit the streetlight, but the driver swerves just in time. Horns blast from other cars as the van careens across the traffic.

"Watch out!" Miss Scarlet yells.

The van has turned too far. It's hurtling towards the concrete barrier that is there to stop cars from falling off the bridge and into the river below.

You brace yourself against the dashboard.

The van smashes into the barrier. Everyone inside lurches sideways. The concrete cracks but doesn't collapse.

"You little—" Miss Scarlet begins.

Before she can finish her sentence, another car slams into the van from behind. Everyone is jolted again. This time the concrete shatters and suddenly the van is falling off the bridge. It's as though gravity has turned upside down. The world spins around you as the van plummets faster and faster.

The last thing you see is the dark river rushing towards you.

SPLASH!

THE END.
To try again, go back to page 80.

07:42

"What's in there?" you ask, as Mr. Signet and Mr. Sharp drag the box through the staff room.

"The end of the world," Mr. Signet says.

Miss Scarlet silences him with a sharp look. "The getaway van should be here in a couple of minutes. Get that out of here."

You risk another glance up — but the man in the shiny clothes is gone. He's disappeared.

Ding! It sounds like a coin striking the wall. Everyone looks towards the sound. But nothing is there.

"What was that?" Mr. Signet says.

Miss Scarlet looks at him and then says, "Where's Alex?"

Mr. Sharp has vanished. You didn't hear him leave and you only took your eyes off him for a second.

Miss Scarlet turns to the open door, leading to the customer area of the bank. "Alex?" she yells.

Silence.

"Where could he . . ." She stops talking when she realizes Mr. Signet has vanished too. Now it's just you and her in the staff room.

Finally realizing that she's under attack, she grabs you by the collar.

"Show yourself," she says, "or the kid gets it. You have five seconds."

Ding! You both turn to face the noise. Again, there's nothing. But when you look back at Miss Scarlet, the weapon has vanished from her hand.

Her face pales. Defenceless, she raises her hands.

"I surrender," she says. "There's no need to—"

This time you do see him — the man in the shiny suit, sprinting impossibly fast on perfectly silent shoes. He whips through the room, slamming Miss Scarlet off her feet. They both disappear.

You're alone.

"Hello?" you say.

There's no reply. The ninja has done his work.

00:00

You survived! There are thirteen other ways to escape the danger — try to find them all!

05:16

"**P**ull over," you say. "I'm going to be sick."

Mr. Signet shrinks away, but Miss Scarlet completely ignores you.

"I'm . . ." You bend over and start retching. You've never done such a great performance. For a second it feels like you might actually be sick.

"Don't stop," Miss Scarlet tells the driver.

"Do it out the window," Mr. Sharp says. You roll down the window next to you.

You stick your head out. The wind buffets your face. There are plenty of other cars around, but there's no way to ask the drivers for help. Not without getting the attention of the robbers.

If you took the bundle of cash from the cart, go to page 97.
If you didn't, go to page 102.

`01:47`

You roll out of the way as the SUV draws nearer. The brakes shriek and the tires squeal. A smell of scorched rubber fills the air.

It's not enough. The half-melted tire rushes towards you—

SCREECH!

THE END.

Go back to page 102 to try again!

03:54

You dig the bundle of cash out of your pocket. There must be five thousand dollars here, at least. Before the robbers can stop you, you rip off the rubber band and chuck the money out the open window.

The bills get picked up by the wind and flutter all over the bridge. Some drift over the edge into the water. A few stick to car windshields. Others fall to the road.

For a second nothing happens.

Then the whole world goes crazy.

Cars screech to a stop all over the bridge. Drivers and passengers leap out. Other cars swerve to avoid them. Suddenly the bridge is a mess of haphazardly parked cars and scurrying pedestrians. You've created an instant traffic jam. There's nowhere for the van to go. The driver slams on the brakes.

You wrench the door open. Mr. Signet tries to grab you, but he's too slow. In a second you're out the door, pushing past greedy people as you sprint across the bridge.

Miss Scarlet takes aim with her laser. She can't let you get away — you're the only one who can identify all the robbers, including the van driver. The road is covered with people. If Miss Scarlet shoots, someone could get hurt. You have to get off this bridge right now . . .

"Freeze!" Miss Scarlet roars.

You dash over to the concrete barrier at the edge of the bridge and leap over it.

As soon as you look down, you realize you've made a terrible mistake. You're hurtling towards the water, twenty or thirty metres up. Can you really survive the impact?

Too late now. You're already falling, faster and faster; the dark water is rushing towards you.

Wham! It's like hitting a hardwood floor. The impact shocks every part of your body and knocks the wind right out of you.

There's no time to recover. Desperately you paddle upwards, fighting the current. Your head breaks the surface and you gasp. Breathing is painful — you think your ribs might be broken. You probably shouldn't have taken that money — but it saved your life.

The river carries you away from the bridge. You're well and truly out of range.

Maybe the robbers got away. Maybe they didn't.

You swim for the distant shore.

00:00
You survived! There are thirteen other ways to escape the danger — try to find them all!

07:42

"You don't need me anymore," you say. "I'll wait with the other hostages."

Miss Scarlet's eyes narrow. "You'll stay exactly where you are," she says.

"Where's Alex?" Mr. Signet says.

You all look around. Mr. Sharp has vanished.

"Alex?" Miss Scarlet calls.

"He was right here," Mr. Signet says.

You glance up. The man in the shiny clothes is still there . . .

And now he's not alone.

Mr. Sharp is stuck to the ceiling by some kind of fast-drying glue. His lips and nostrils are sealed shut with the same substance. His eyes are bulging. He can't breathe.

It seems impossible for the man to have grabbed Mr. Sharp and glued him to the ceiling so quickly without making a sound, in a room full of people. But there's no other explanation.

Miss Scarlet turns to you. You look down just in time.

"You know something," she says. "What did they say to you on the phone?"

"What do you mean?" you ask innocently.

There's a pause as Miss Scarlet weighs her options.

"Zachary," she says finally. "Deal with the kid."

Mr. Signet pulls a knife off his belt. He approaches you. You look up. The man in the shiny clothes — the ninja — has vanished.

Miss Scarlet walks over to the metal box. A keypad is mounted on the side. You watch as she types in the letters *ANNM*.

You hold up your hands. Your heart is racing. "Wait," you tell Mr. Signet. "You don't need to do this."

He grins, showing big, blunt teeth—

Then he falls over, unconscious.

Miss Scarlet immediately scrambles into a corner, where the ninja can't sneak up on her. She scans the room, but can't see anyone. Nor can you. The ninja has vanished again.

"Whoever you are," she shouts, "you know what's in this box. Millions of nanobots that can build absolutely anything. I've just programmed them to make forty kilos of ammonium nitrate. Enough to turn this whole city block to ash."

You back away, slowly.

"So you have a choice," Miss Scarlet continues. "You can chase me, or you can stop the nanobots from completing the bomb. You have thirty seconds."

She runs out the door.

You look around.

Still no sign of the man in the shiny clothes. Maybe

he's already chased after her. Maybe he was gone before she made her threat.

If you try to disarm the bomb, go to page 82.
If you run for your life, go to page 103.

03:54

The van moves slowly through the heavy traffic. You watch the pavement cruising past below. If you jumped out at this speed, what would happen? Bruises, definitely. Broken bones, maybe. But death? Probably not — assuming you get clear of the wheels.

Before you have an opportunity to rethink this, you launch yourself out the window.

The robbers yell in surprise as you flop out of the van and fall towards the road. You shield your face as you hit the pavement. The impact grazes your hands and knees, but you don't think anything is broken.

The van hits the brakes and stops a few metres away. The door slides open. But you have bigger problems. An SUV is hurtling towards you.

You try to roll out of the way, but the car is coming too fast. The man driving sees you and stamps on the brakes.

Either he will stop in time, or he won't.

It's a fifty-fifty shot.

Turn to page 96 . . .

. . . or page 105.

04:21

You sprint out of the staff room and into the customer area of the bank. The hostages are already gone. The police must have evacuated them when the ninja came in.

The front door is unlocked. You dash out. It's pandemonium outside. Police rush back and forth, tending to hostages, checking exits, struggling to keep news crews behind the crime scene tape.

Miss Scarlet is running towards a gap in the cordon. The ninja is right behind her, his silver clothes shimmering in the daylight. He's catching up to her.

"Run!" you yell. "There's a bomb! The bank is going to blow up!"

A cop tries to grab your arm. You duck around him and keep running. "Get out of here!" you yell.

The ninja tackles Miss Scarlet. They both hit the ground. "You fool!" she screams. "You were supposed to stop the bomb!"

The ninja sprays her face with some kind of aerosol can, gluing her mouth shut.

You keep running—

And then there's a tremendous *kaboom*. The shockwave knocks you off your feet. You hit the ground, hard.

The sky goes dark as the bank is vaporized. A hurricane of concrete dust scours the street. Bricks and blocks rain down.

You try to scream, but the storm swallows you up.

THE END.

To try again, go back to page 85.

01:47

You roll desperately across the road, ignoring the pain in your joints. The pavement jars your elbows. The SUV twists sideways as the driver fights to keep it from going into a skid. The tire rolls towards your face—

It hits you.

But not hard. The hot rubber bumps your forehead as the SUV finally stops. You find yourself looking up at the grimy underside of the car and smelling the oil in the engine.

Someone grabs your ankles and drags you out from under the vehicle.

It's Mr. Sharp. He looms over you, his face red with fury. Miss Scarlet is pointing the laser at you.

"Wait," you say.

She squeezes the trigger.

Zap!

The laser beam just barely misses you. Miss Scarlet falls over, her limbs rigid. So does Mr. Sharp. They twitch on the ground. After a second you notice the crackling wires sticking out of their bodies.

Two police officers approach, both holding tasers. They check the pulses of the two robbers before they turn to you.

"Are you OK, kid?" one of the officers asks.

You try to speak, but your throat closes up. You're crying. The robbery, the kidnapping, the car crash, the laser — it's all too much.

"It's OK," the officer says. "Let's get you home."

00:00

You survived! There are thirteen other ways to escape the danger — try to find them all!

23:01

"**Y**ou don't understand," you tell the cop. "They were clearly robbers. They were wearing ski masks. One of them had a weapon. Another one had a pair of bolt cutters."

The police officer looks taken aback. But he still doesn't go towards the bank.

"You swear all this is true?" he says.

You nod, not trusting yourself to speak.

"OK," he says. "I'll call for backup. You come with me."

He leads you over to his patrol car. He talks into his radio as he walks. "Dispatch, I have an unconfirmed report of three armed men and one woman running into HBS bank on Collins Street. Please send all available units to investigate."

He opens the car door. You climb in. He shuts the door and hops into the driver's seat.

Metal mesh separates you from him. It makes you feel like a criminal.

"Where are we going?" you ask.

He starts the engine and pulls away from the curb. "Back to the station," he says. "I'll take a full statement there."

Out the window, the streets roll past. Quiet and safe.

You'd never think a robbery was happening nearby.

Maybe it isn't. Those four people might just have needed to make an urgent deposit. You hope you haven't made a terrible mistake by lying to the officer.

But they did look very suspicious. The woman had a look in her eyes, a look which—

Something occurs to you.

"How did you know about the woman?" you ask.

"Sorry?" he asks.

"You said three men and one woman. How did you know?"

"You told me."

"No, I didn't."

"I'm pretty sure you did," he says.

When he was talking on the radio, you didn't hear anyone respond. Was the radio even switched on?

You check the doors. They're locked.

If you pretend to remember telling him about the woman, go to the next page.

If you ask him to pull over, go to page 112.

15:25

"Oh yeah," you say, hiding your fear. "I did say 'she.' I forgot."

The cop says nothing. It's impossible to tell if he believes you, but now you're sure something's not right. Is he a real police officer, bribed by the robbers? Or is he a thug in a fake uniform?

The patrol car seems real. The mesh is securely bolted in place. The windows are extra-thick glass, making the traffic outside eerily silent. There's no way to wind the window down. This is where suspects sit after they've been arrested. It's designed to be escape-proof.

You glance at the mirror. The cop — or whoever he is — watches the road, not you.

You have one advantage. Most suspects would be handcuffed, but you're not. Maybe there are things you could reach that they couldn't.

In some cars, a concealed trap door leads through the back seat into the trunk. You check the seat. Yes, there's the trap door — but it's been stitched shut. Maybe all police cars are like that.

The cop's eyes flick to yours in the mirror. "You OK back there?" he asks.

Stifling your growing panic, you nod.

He turns back to the road.

Something gleams on the floor. You lean down. An old utility knife. Maybe a suspect ditched it here, knowing they would be searched when they got to jail.

You pick it up and start slicing through the stitches, keeping one eye on the cop. Every time he glances over, you hide the tool behind your palm and act casual.

Soon the trap door is free. The patrol car stops at an intersection. You wait for the green light.

When the car pulls into the intersection and the cop is most distracted, you pull open the trap door, crawl through and tug it closed behind you.

The trunk is hot and dark. And empty, as far as you can tell. There isn't even a toolbox. Just a lever that will probably open the trunk if you pull it.

It doesn't take the cop long to notice that you're gone. He yells, "What the—" and slams on the brakes. The car stops so suddenly that you nearly roll over.

If you open the trunk and run for it, go to page 114.
If you stay hidden, go to page 116.

23:01

"OK," you say. "Thanks for your, uh, help."

The cop watches you walk back towards the bank. You turn left before you get there, as though you're going somewhere else. You walk around to the other side of the building, out of the officer's sight.

This is the back of the bank. A frosted window is above you, just out of reach. There's a fire door, which will certainly be locked, or at least alarmed.

You try the handle anyway. The door swings open.

You step back, startled. This is a bank. Who would leave the back door unlocked? It's proof that something strange is happening — although you're still hoping the robbers are just suspicious-looking customers.

There's no alarm, so you slip inside.

You find yourself in a concrete stairwell. Giant cardboard boxes sit in the corner. Some are open, revealing disassembled office chairs and foam padding. There are stairs leading to a security door with a keycard scanner.

You hear footsteps. Someone is coming towards you, fast. And you're definitely not supposed to be here.

If you hide in one of the big cardboard boxes, turn to page 127.

If you try the security door, go to page 129.

15:25

"**P**ull over," you say.

The cop glances at you in the mirror. "Why?"

"I need to get out," you say. "I get carsick."

"We're almost there," the cop says.

You look around. This is an industrial district, full of mechanics' workshops and self-storage rental places. "Almost where?" you say.

He takes a right-hand turn towards a warehouse. Rusted cars are parked haphazardly all around it. You can't see any people. Twisted metal is stacked in the corners.

The cop stops the car. "Stay here," he says.

"Can you open the window at least?" you ask.

"I'll be right back."

He walks away across the parking lot, leaving you in the stifling car.

You scoot across the back seat and try the opposite door. It's locked too.

You dig your phone out of your pocket and dial emergency services. This time the call goes through. Whatever was blocking the signal before, it's gone now.

The phone rings and rings.

Finally someone answers. "Police, fire or ambulance?"

"Police," you say. "I'm—"

Something slams into the car from above. You scream as a gargantuan metal claw crushes the roof. Steel blades slice inwards from all angles. A crane lifts the car off the ground.

"Help me!" you shout. "Somebody help!"

But you can't even hear yourself over the sound of the claw. Tortured metal shrieks as the car rises higher and higher. Hydraulics hiss. The car crumples in towards you.

If you try to break the window with your elbow, go to page 124.

If you duck under the blades and crouch in the footwell, go to page 126.

10:45

You pull the lever. The trunk pops open. You scramble out and land in a crouch on the road. The foul-smelling exhaust washes over you, making you dizzy. A car screeches to a halt and honks its horn as you sprint across the road, desperate to get out of sight.

"Stop right there!" the cop yells. He leaps out of the car and runs after you.

You don't stop. There's a shopping centre up ahead. No one will stop him from grabbing you — you're a kid and he looks like a cop — but maybe you can lose him in the crowd.

"The kid's packing heat!" yells the cop.

Shrieks fill the air. People scatter. A customer over-turns one of the outdoor tables and cowers behind it. You can hear the cop's footsteps getting closer and closer.

"He's lying. He's not a real cop!" you shout. "Someone help!"

But people just run the other way. No one comes to your aid.

You sprint through the glass doors into the shopping centre. People are looking in shiny shop windows. The air is thick with laughter and conversation and pop hits from the nineties. No one in here has noticed the commotion outside yet.

You dash across the polished floor to an escalator and run down it.

"Stop that kid!" the cop is yelling. But no one is quick enough to grab you.

You leap over the rubber handrail and fall a couple of metres before your feet hit the floor, hard. Your shoes squeak as you sprint around the corner.

If you go left, towards the elevator, turn to page 117.
If you go right, towards the bathrooms, turn to page 119.

10:45

You lie perfectly still in the trunk as the cop opens his door. You can hear him walking around the vehicle, muttering to himself, probably staring at the surrounding streets and wondering where you've gone.

Hopefully he will assume that you opened the door somehow and ran across the street to the shopping centre. It looked crowded when you saw it out the window.

But then he might decide just to drive away, with you still trapped in the trunk. Then what?

"You can't have gone far," the cop mutters.

You hold your breath.

The trunk opens. The sunrise dazzles you. The cop is looming there, holding a spray can. There is a look of grim satisfaction on his face.

"Not far at all," he says and sprays a mist into your face.

You suddenly feel like you're falling. You try to climb out of the trunk, but already your limbs won't obey your brain. A dark cloud settles over you before you can make a sound.

THE END.

Go back to page 107 to try again.

06:27

You run left, towards the row of elevators and slam your hand against the call button. How long will it take for an elevator to arrive? Will you have time to get out of sight before the cop comes down the escalator?

You press the button again. A second later, one of the doors opens. You duck in and select a floor at random — *B4 PARKING*. The parking lot four levels below ground.

The doors start to close. But just when you think you're safe, a hand snakes in and stops them. The cop pushes his way into the elevator, glowering at you.

You can't step around him. You're trapped.

He points a futuristic-looking laser at you and waits for the doors to close. No witnesses.

"You're making a mistake," you say desperately. "The shopping centre is full of cameras. If you hurt me, you'll be caught."

He doesn't look worried. The doors close.

"Seriously. There's a camera right above your head," you say.

He falls for it. When he glances up, you lunge forwards and try to rip the laser from his grip. But he's holding it too tightly. *Blam! Blam!* Laser beams burn holes in the ceiling. *Blam!* The sound is deafening in the enclosed car. *Blam!* You wrestle for control of the laser.

The blasts shred the ceiling and everything above it. The cables. The brakes.

Suddenly the elevator is falling. You're weightless, fighting a criminal in mid-air while the elevator plummets down and down towards—

WHAM!

THE END.

To try again, go back to page 107.

06:27

You duck into the shopping centre bathrooms, hoping the cop didn't see you. Sometimes public bathrooms have a fire exit at the back — but not this one. There are just polished mirrors, a row of cubicles and an overpowering smell of bleach.

You run into one of the cubicles and lock the door. Then you climb over the wall into the next cubicle. Hopefully the cop will assume you're behind the locked door and you can sneak out past him. You hide behind the half-closed door of your cubicle.

Shoes clack into the bathroom. Someone's here. The cop?

He walks past your cubicle and stops at the one with the locked door.

"I know you're in there," he says. "Come on out."

You stay silent.

"Resisting arrest is a very serious offence," he says. "But if you turn yourself in now, we can pretend you stayed in the car."

"That's him!" cries a voice.

The cop grunts. There's a buzzing sound, like a faulty light bulb, and then a *thump*.

You peek out the door. Two police officers, a man and

a woman, are standing over the fake cop. The woman is holding a taser.

"That's the guy who stole your car?" she asks the policeman.

He nods. "We'll have to try to figure out what he was planning."

"He was the lookout," you say, your voice wavering as you step out of the cubicle.

The policewoman's eyes widen. "Who are you?"

"I was at the HBS bank," you say. "On Collins Street. I saw — I mean, I *think* I saw a bank robbery. This guy was supposed to stop any real police from turning up, I guess."

The man laughs. "Well, he did a lousy job. We caught all three robbers and rescued all the hostages."

"Come on, kid," the woman says. "Let's get you a hot chocolate and you can tell us what you know."

You exhale. It looks like everything worked out OK.

00:00

You survived! There are thirteen other ways to escape the danger — try to find them all!

20:59

"**B**rianna," you say.

"And your last name?" Miss Scarlet demands.

"Brianna Catton," you stammer.

"Hmm." You're not sure if she believes you.

"Brianna Elaine Catton," you say. "I go to school at—"

She cuts you off. "I need a favour, Brianna."

You look at Kye. He looks as perplexed and terrified as you.

"The building is locked down," Miss Scarlet says. "Any minute now, the police will call. I need someone to talk to them for me."

She pauses, as if waiting for you to speak. You open your mouth, then you close it again.

"You're going to say exactly what I tell you to," Miss Scarlet continues. "Otherwise . . ." She points the laser at Kye. Her finger is on the trigger. He trembles.

"I'll do whatever you want," you say quickly. "You don't have to hurt anybody."

Miss Scarlet smiles. "Good girl. I'll be back in a moment."

She and Mr. Sharp walk over to the counter, out of sight. You can hear them talking to someone, but can't make out the words.

While they're distracted, you scan your surroundings, looking for a way out. The air conditioner catches your eye. The brackets are loose and the bolts are scattered on the floor. The vent behind it looks just big enough to crawl through.

Can you and the other hostages get out of sight before the bad guys come back?

If you try to escape through the vent, go to page 12.

If you don't risk it, go to page 16.

01:04

You are vaporized.

A split second later, so is Kye.

The nanobots sizzle away into harmless flakes of charcoal. The water in the sewer turns to steam as the shockwave flashes outwards through the sewer tunnels. Manhole covers explode upwards all along the street. Up above, the bank is rocked by the explosion. The police behind the cordon throw themselves to the ground and cover their faces as debris rains down.

Inside the vault, the device — the completed bomb — falls from Miss Scarlet's hands and shatters.

The police recover quickly and storm into the building. The hostages are rescued. The robbers are arrested. Alhamed is congratulated for his heroism.

The world is safe. But you and Kye are dust.

THE END.

To try again, go back to page 24.

08:59

You slam your elbow against the window.

"Ow!" Your elbow is in agony, but the window is completely unharmed.

Wild with terror, you pound your fists against the glass. It's no use. You can't break it.

The massive metal claws crush the car, bit by bit. Then the window cracks under the pressure.

You punch the glass with renewed desperation. Chunks pop out and fall to the gravel far below.

You clear out the last of the glass and pull your shoulders through the window. The car is crumpling behind you, getting smaller and smaller around your kicking feet. You drag your legs out just in time.

But now you're dangling from a car window frame at least ten metres above the ground. The evil cop is nowhere to be seen. The claw that crushed the car hangs from a crane. The only sound is the creaking and groaning of the cable above you.

You hang in terrified silence for a few minutes. Your hands and arms are starting to hurt, but you can't see a way down.

Suddenly you spot a guy in a neon vest inside the control cabin of the crane.

"Hey!" you call out.

He peers at you from under his hard hat. "What are you doing up there?" he shouts.

"Help me!" you shout. "I can't hold on much longer!"

"Don't worry, kid," he says, fiddling with the controls. "I'll get you down."

After what seems like a long time, the crane whines and starts to lower the car.

As you descend towards the ground, your eyes turn to the horizon. The bank stands tall amongst the other buildings in the distance. A helicopter is landing on the roof.

Your feet touch the ground and you scramble out of the way so the crane can put down the half-crushed car. You're safe now, but Kye might not be. You wonder what's going on inside the bank. Did the robbers get caught? If only there was some way to find out . . .

00:00

You survived! There are thirteen other ways to escape the danger — try to find them all!

08:59

You scramble into the footwell and curl into a ball, just in time. The claws rip and tear through the car above you, tearing your shirt.

Then they stop. Silence falls, except for the ringing in your ears. The top half of the car is crushed in the grip of the claw, but the bottom half is mostly intact. You're safe.

The car lurches sideways. The crane that picked it up whines as it rotates. Hopefully the claw will lower the car to another part of the lot and you can find a way out.

The windows have smashed under the pressure, but the frames have folded into themselves. You can't see where the crane is taking you. You wonder if the corrupt cop is controlling it, or if it's just a regular crane operator, unaware that you're inside.

The crane stops. The car sways sickeningly from side to side. Silence again.

And then the claw opens up, dropping the car.

SMASH!

THE END.

Go back to page 107 to try again.

21:50

You race over to one of the big cardboard boxes, pull out half a chair to make room and scramble inside. It's not as roomy as it looked. There's barely enough space to close the lid over your head.

The footsteps get closer and closer. They stop right next to the box.

There's a pause. You hold your breath and wonder what the person — security guard, or bank manager, or whoever it is — is thinking. Did he or she hear you enter the stairwell? Are they wondering why a piece of an office chair is lying on the floor, or noticing that the box is now closed?

A huge hand plunges into the box and grabs you. You scream as the hand drags you to your feet. You find yourself face to face with one of the strangers from the van — the man with the knife tattoo — you call him Mr. Sharp in your head.

"You're coming with me," he says.

He shifts a stack of boxes, revealing a narrow corridor you didn't see before. Then he drags you along it and through a door marked *STAFF ONLY*. You emerge into the main area of the bank, where four customers are huddled in the corner. One of them is Kye. His head is down and his hands are shaking.

The red-headed woman with the scar — Miss Scarlet, you find yourself calling her — stands nearby, threatening them with some kind of futuristic weapon. It looks like a laser from a sci-fi movie.

The window above the counter is mostly covered by a security shutter, but there's a gap at the top. A hole has been cut through the exposed glass.

Your heart is pounding. This is definitely a bank robbery — and now you're a prisoner of the robbers.

There's no sign of the man with the overalls and the silver tooth, or the one with the signet ring. You wonder where they've gone.

"Got another hostage for you," says Mr. Sharp.

"Sit over there," Miss Scarlet tells you, pointing. "*Away* from the air conditioning unit. What's your name, kid?"

If you say "Jacob," go to page 3.
If you say "Brianna," go to page 121.

21:50

You try the handle. The security door hasn't been closed properly, so it swings open. Unable to believe your luck, you dart through and pull it closed behind you. The lock beeps and a red light blinks on next to the door. You have a feeling you won't be able to come back this way.

You're not sure what you expected the inside of a bank to look like, but it's not this. The walls and floor are covered with polished white tiles. The lights are painfully bright overhead. A computer sits on a stainless steel bench next to a giant microscope. There are no people. This place looks like a science lab.

The door handle behind you rattles. The door is locked, but whoever is following you knows which way you went and they might have a keycard.

You look around for somewhere to hide. There's a small, dark room to your right — a storage room, or maybe an office. You duck inside and close the airtight metal door. It seals you in with a hiss.

A gas-like smell hangs in the air. There is a thick glass window near the door, but it's too narrow to let in much light. The room is bare except for a steel box and an unsettlingly lifelike doll. The doll sits upright on the floor in the centre of the room. It wears a cotton onesie and a baby bonnet. Its realistic blue eyes don't move but still seem to follow you as you search the room for somewhere to hide.

There's nowhere. You try to open the steel box, but it's tightly sealed. A keypad is fixed to the side.

A light snaps on above you.

"Any explosive compounds left in the air?" a woman is saying. Her voice is muffled by the window.

"Less than two percent," a man says. "The nanobots consumed most of the flammable gases before they returned to the box."

"And what about the doll? Did they make it to our specifications?"

"I haven't checked yet. Let's take a look."

Your heart beats faster as you realize that they're headed for the room that you're in. Before you can crouch under the window, two faces appear on the other side of the glass. A woman and a man, both wearing lab coats, stare at you.

"Hey!" the man says. "How did you get in there?"

You raise your hands. You're busted. "I came in looking for my friend," you say. "I'm sorry — I thought the bank was getting robbed."

It doesn't sound believable out loud.

"Incredible," the woman says. "It's so lifelike!"

You look down at the doll, which hasn't moved.

It takes you a second to realize the woman is talking about you.

"You think . . ." the man begins.

"I think we should be more careful when programming the nanobots," the woman says excitedly. "They haven't just created a toy. They've made an artificial life form! A moving, breathing, talking person!"

This must be some kind of prank. You reach for the airtight metal door. The woman locks it before you get there, sealing you in with the doll and the box.

"It's even trying to escape," the woman says. "I've always said it was possible for the nanobots to create life — but I didn't expect it to happen so soon!"

"I just walked in," you say, starting to panic.

"It could be telling the truth," the man says. He sounds doubtful, and he's still referring to you as "it."

"How?" The woman points at the security door you came in through. "The door is locked. And this lab is hidden in the staff area of a bank. People can't just wander in. Besides, someone would have told us if there was a robbery going on downstairs."

The man looks you up and down, becoming convinced. "It's so realistic," he says. "How did this happen?"

"Let's find out," the woman says. "Instruct the nanobots to disassemble it so we can see the insides."

"Disassemble what?" you say.

Ignoring you, the man walks over to the computer and types in a password.

"Disassemble what?" you say again.

The woman ignores you. The man keeps typing.

Behind you, the steel box opens.

A grey cloud emerges from inside. It looks like smoke at first — then it starts to shimmer. It floats towards you, as though it can smell your terror.

If you try to cancel the man's instructions using the keypad on the side of the steel box, go to the next page.

If you pick up the box and use it to try and break the window and escape, go to page 136.

05:41

You dodge around the shimmering grey cloud and run over to the steel box. There's a little screen above the keypad which reads *OPERATION IN PROGRESS*.

You look for a cancel button. There isn't one.

You push the *ESCAPE* key.

A message flashes on the screen: *ACCESS DENIED*.

You try *CTRL+ALT+DEL*.

ACCESS DENIED.

The cloud lands on your back like a million flies. Your skin starts to tingle, then to sting.

These must be the nanobots.

"No!" you shriek, trying to shake them off. The cloud only becomes thicker.

In desperation, you wrench the keypad off the box, hoping to use it like a flyswatter—

Then you see the circuitry underneath. Maybe you can use it to stop the nanobots.

It's not like the movies. There's no manual override button. But there is a nine-volt battery.

In science class, you once got shocked by one of these. The teacher told you to lick your thumb and touch the prongs. The saliva completed the circuit, so the battery zapped you.

The scientists' voices echo through your mind. *... Any explosive compounds left in the air? ... Less than two percent.*

Can you use electricity to start a fire and fry the nanobots? It's an insane plan. You're likely to blow yourself up. But you have to do something — and fast.

You rip the battery out of the casing and lick your thumb. As your wet skin approaches the prongs, a blue flash lances out.

The spark is tiny, but it's enough. Your hand turns into a fireball as the flammable gas in the air ignites. You scream as the flames shoot outward—

Knocking the nanobots stone dead. The grey cloud drops suddenly, silently, to the floor. Flakes of it fall from your back like dandruff.

As quickly as it appeared, the fire is gone. The gas has all burned up, leaving only air. Your whole body hurts. The air feels like ice. But you're alive.

The door opens. The man runs in and falls to his knees amongst the dead nanobots. "My babies!" he screams.

"Pull yourself together." The woman walks in behind him. "We have plenty more in the vault."

The man chokes back a sob.

"I just got a call from downstairs," the woman continues. "The police are arresting three bank robbers right now." She glares at you. "It looks like it was telling the truth after all."

You should be furious but all you feel is relief.

The woman digs a cloth from her pocket and pours a bitter-smelling substance onto it.

"So . . . I can go?" you say.

She nods. "Right after the memory wipe."

"Memory what?"

She presses the damp cloth over your face. The world goes fuzzy.

00:00

You survived! There are thirteen other ways to escape the danger — try to find them all!

05:41

You grab the sides of the box and pull. It's heavier than you expected. For a horrifying second you think you won't be able to move it. Then you adjust your grip and the adrenalin kicks in. You haul the box to the window.

The deadly grey cloud swirls around you. Flecks of it settle on your face and hands. At first they just tingle. Then they start to sting, like biting insects. These must be the nanobots.

You reach the window. Sweat pouring from your brow, straining like a weightlifter, you raise the box.

Your skin feels like it's on fire. You'll only get one chance at this. With the last of your strength, you hurl the box at the window.

Thunk! The steel bounces off the thick glass without leaving a scratch. The box thuds to the floor.

"No!" you shriek.

Your last thought is that no one will ever know what happened to you.

THE END.

Go back to page 111 to try again.

15:15

"It's 137!" you cry. "Don't hurt anyone. The code is right there on a sticky note!"

Miss Scarlet looks at where you're pointing. She chuckles. "Huh. Did none of you think to search the room?"

She didn't think of it either, but none of the other robbers says so.

"We didn't think they'd be dumb enough to write it down," Mr. Sharp grumbles.

Miss Scarlet punches in the new code.

You hold your breath.

The keypad beeps and the bolts withdraw. Mr. Signet hauls the door open.

"Well done, kid," Miss Scarlet tells you. "You saved your friends' lives . . . for now."

"You can just let us go," you say. "We'll sneak out the back way. The cops will think you still have hostages. You'll still get what you want."

She shoots you a thin smile. "Nice try. The building must be surrounded by now—but soon that won't matter."

The inside of the vault has bare concrete walls, a concrete ceiling and laminated tiles that probably cover a concrete floor. You expected to see piles of gold, or at least cash, but there's only a big metal box in the middle of the floor, about the size of a desk. Maybe banks don't store much real money in them these days. It's all electronic. But if that's the case, what are the robbers here to steal?

Miss Scarlet answers your unspoken question by kneeling next to the metal box. She holds her hands out but doesn't touch it. It's as though she's warming them by a campfire.

"The jammer will keep us safe, right?" Mr. Sharp says nervously. "When the signal goes out?"

Miss Scarlet ignores him.

"Relax," Mr. Signet tells Mr. Sharp. "Only working phones will explode. Stay close to the jammer and you'll be fine."

You start to feel dizzy. Whatever is in this box, it sounds like it's going to hurt people. Maybe a lot of people.

Miss Scarlet stands up. She looks at her watch. "Where's my phone call?" she asks.

Boom! The whole building shakes. The lights flicker. It's as though an asteroid has hit the roof.

"Looks like the police decided to skip the phone call," Mr. Signet yells.

While they're distracted, you lean over to the box. A screen glows on the side of the box. It reads *SET:* _ _ _ _ _. A keypad waits underneath. You don't know the right code this time.

Maybe this is the first time the box has been used. Maybe you could set a password. Something they would never guess.

If you type in your own name, go to page 61.

If you type in RHINOCEROS, go to page 61.

If you type in BEEHIVE, go to page 61.

COUNTDOWN TO EVEN MORE DANGER . . .

Can you survive the
BULLET TRAIN DISASTER
and **SHOCKWAVE**?

30 MINUTES. 30 ENDINGS.
YOU CHOOSE
IF YOU LIVE OR DIE.